Always a Bridesmaid...

This book is dedicated to all the women students I've known over the years who have handled their business in undergraduate and graduate school.

Always
a Bridesmaid...

Copyright © 2014 by Karen Sloan-Brown

This book is printed on acid-free paper.

ISBN: 978-0-9915517-6-7

Library of Congress Cataloging-in-Publication Data on file.

Editor: Cornelius Brown

Acknowledgments
Thank all of my friends and fellow students
for sharing their experiences with me.

1

Chapter One

"**I** know that's not my alarm clock ringing this early, the devil is a sho-nuff liar," I muttered to myself as I turned over on my side still half-sleep. I felt like I had just lain down. I rose up on my elbow to clear my head and shut down the noise and that's when I realized that it was my cell phone ringing. "Who in the hell is calling me," I fussed as I leaned closer to see the clock on my nightstand. The glowing red LED lights shone 5:00 AM.

"Oh, Jesus," I said, flustered with fear rushing to my heart as my senses came to me. In one swift motion I grabbed my phone, praying fervently that it wasn't a family emergency at home and that my mama was good. Half scared I answered, "Hello."

"Guess who's walking down the aisle next, girlfriend?" Yvonne sang excitedly into the phone as soon as I picked up.

"I know you didn't just call me at the crack of dawn," I snapped, falling back on my pillow irritated and relieved at the same time. "Girl, do you know what time it is? Some of us have things to do and need our sleep."

"Forget some sleep, I wanted you to be the first to know that

Greg proposed and I said yes, I'm looking at my ring right now."

"Lucky me, and I suppose this news couldn't have waited like another hour or two," I said sarcastically.

"Uh-uh, Tia, no it couldn't. Do you know how long I've waited for this man to pop the question? Don't you know how much drama he put me through? Seriously, and I am not about to let you rain on my future wedding."

"Bring it down two notches, Yvonne, don't get super dramatic. I'm sorry, and congratulations on your engagement," I said, resigning myself to the inevitable and joining the celebration.

"Now you know I want you to be one of my bridesmaids," she said with her jubilation rising back up to ten. "We are going to do this thing right. I want to be married within the next sixty days. I'm not taking any chances on waiting and something or someone getting in the mix and keeping me from tying this knot."

"You know I'm here for you, girl, but I've got my own plans that need to jump off in the next sixty days. Plus I have a long day ahead of me and I need some more sleep before I get started with it. I'll definitely call you later when I get a break," I promised, looking sadly at the clock knowing I barely had one hour before the real alarm went off.

I didn't get much sleep after Yvonne's wake-up call. That was all I needed to hear, another one of my girls calling to announce the good news that she's getting married and requesting my presence in the wedding ceremony as yet again, a bridesmaid. I have been in four wedding in the last eighteen months. Now don't get me wrong I love my girls and I am happy for them, but I've been standing in line for a while now and I'm sure I should be next. How many people are in this line, and how long do I have to wait for my turn at the altar?

I've listened to Pastor Andrews tell me, "Let the man find you, and don't go chasing every Tim, James, and Larry." I've been patient, knowing you can't rush a good thing, but my future man is still missing in action. What is the hold up? Now, I must admit that I have answered my share of wrong numbers, entertained a few possibilities, but my Prince has not come, not even his valet, and I'm starting to get an attitude.

Before I go any further, let me formally introduce myself. My name is Tia King, I am a southern girl, born and bred in the Music City, country music that is, Nashville, Tennessee. I'm a thirty-three year old, and I'll try not to brag, milk chocolate brown with dark eyes, shoulder length black hair, kinda cute with fuller figure curves that deserve a danger sign, intellectual, hell of a cook, "bad –to-the-bone" black woman. I love my daddy, but I am a straight-up mama's girl. I have done everything she's told me, made good grades, gone to college, kept my legs closed as much as possible, and paid some portion of my tithes. I also have a brother, Thomas, who has four children minus his wife, who love and worry their auntie to death.

I was the first one in my family to graduate from college and now after eleven years of educating myself I'm close to earning my Ph.D at Tennessee State University. There is no way you could convince some of my ghetto cousins that I can't walk on water and this was no time for them to watch me drown and learn the truth.

I've been studying Cell Biology for almost seven years and

for some reason the last semester has been like dragging a stubborn mule to run in the Kentucky Derby. The race to finish before my money runs out is in a dead heat. One important thing I've learned while completing my studies, even if it was a little late, is that medical research is without a shadow of a doubt the lowest paying job with the highest requirements of education and expertise in the country. I'm about to get my Ph.D. and I'm living well below the poverty level according to the numbers for a family of four. Now I may not be a family of four, but my landlord, my cell phone service provider, high-ass Comcast, and the electric company have not got the newsflash.

My third objective in my research has been completed so I'm nearing the finish line. It's time for me to make a move, several in fact. I need to graduate, find a job, meet my soul mate, and fulfill my destiny. I know that sounds like a challenging "to do" list, but I have the confidence of Martin Luther King, and I shall overcome. I've read all the magazine articles that have said the odds of me as a black woman finding a man who will commit are nil or next to none, but hey, they don't know me. I've been in school long enough to learn that any successful venture requires a well-thought-out plan and I know better than to pursue anything without the proper preparation.

My mind, body, and soul must be in synch, working as a fine-tuned machine. Presently, my mind is clicking on all cylinders, going a mile a minute, and truly my soul is anchored in the Lord, but my body is somewhat of a work in progress. I must confess that what I told you about my curves was a little understated; some might say they are more like mountains. Anyway, I'm always up for a challenge and if Muhammad won't come to the mountain, then the mountain is going to get in the path of Muhammad. Fulfilling my wish list is going to be my own personal expedition, hell, it will be my great adventure.

Renewing my commitment to my own plans gives me the strength to drag myself out of bed. I take a quick shower, pull my hair in a pony-tail, and throw on the uniform of most graduate students, jeans, a t-shirt, and some comfortable sneakers. We work long hours in the labs so trying to be cute is not always practical.

I live in an apartment complex in the Germantown district. It's about a thirty minute healthy walk from campus, even though I always insist on driving. My most loyal friend is my 1994 Toyota Camry, we have been through some things but she has never put me down. I unlock the door and before I can get in I see a twenty dollar bill hanging from the driver's side visor. I snatch it down and slip in it my jeans pocket before I reach in my bag for my cell phone.

"Good morning to you too, Wayne," I said, smiling through the phone, "Thank you for looking out for me, but your lady might not appreciate it."

"No problem, you're always going to be my boo," he said, making my smile even bigger.

"No, I won't," I told him laughing, "My new man better not catch you going into my car."

"I'm not worried; I'm the only man for you. When are you gonna realize that?"

Shaking my head, I hang up the phone. Wayne is one of my ex-boyfriends; he lives in the building right across the street

from me. We get along great since we split up and he helps me
out with odds and ends from time to time, like a little lunch
money in the glove compartment or either putting a few gallons
of gas in my car. The main problem with Wayne is that he was,
for the lack of a better description, too dumb for me. I know
that may sound like I'm a little uppity or bourgeoisie, but
you don't know him. He can't speak three sentences without
assaulting the English language. Outside of the bedroom
we didn't have anything to talk about. I also have three step
children out of the deal who refuse to accept the fact that I am
no longer with their dad.

I met Wayne when I was working at Sally's Beauty Supply
in my undergrad years. He came in to buy some products to
dye his hair blonde. He wasn't in school and he didn't have a
regular job. He was self-employed selling boot-leg CDs and
DVDs, but he was one of those nice kinds of guys who'll give
you the shirt off his back if you ask for it.

I notice the time when I turn up the radio and it's after
nine. I'm going to be late again and I need to stop for some
breakfast because I've got to have my protein and carbs to keep
my energy up for my new mission. I don't know why I drive
an extra ten minutes away from the campus just to get a big
delicious and satisfying bacon and egg sandwich when I should
just grab some fruit at farmer's market across the street. I guess
I'm just not good at self-deprivation.

Finally I make it into the research building and I'm trying to
enjoy my sandwich at my desk in our lab suite but somebody
is blowing up my phone; it has beeped at least four times. I
check the number and it's Dr. Lee, my mentor. He's Chinese

and there is a definite culture clash. I am not ready for this; it is too early in the morning. I know he wants to remind me that we have got to meet and discuss my progress. I'm on my way, but my first stop after I eat and make an appearance in the lab is to go and see my homegirl, Denise.

We go way back as lab mates in our undergrad years at TSU, not to mention, I was also a bridesmaid in her wedding almost three years ago. She graduated last year and accepted a post-doc position in the department. She eventually wants to move further away from Nashville for a fresh perspective so we still have that goal in common.

"Hey girl," I said as I walked in. "I guess you heard about Yvonne's wedding."

"Oh yeah, who hasn't heard," she said jokingly, setting down a rack full of samples. "She texted me last night right in the middle of me and Andre getting busy."

"Personally, I'm tired of buying all these ugly dresses and standing up in all these ghetto weddings for y'all, its payback time for me," I said in a huff.

"Calm down, sister-girl, if you weren't so picky you could find somebody too, you've had more men than all of us put together," she said, laughing.

"Excuse me, I don't see the humor in that and it's not that I'm picky, I just don't want to settle. I don't see why I have to," I said, giving her a little attitude.

"Because you want a man," she snickered, and I had to laugh too.

"I'm for real," I said, "I'm getting ready to turn my focus on graduating, finding a good job, and then a good man."

"Seriously, Tia, that sounds like a plan to me. I need to up my game too; I've got to get a better job. I can barely pay my student loans, so you know I'm down. Opportunity is all about networking," she explained. "You set up a page on Linked-in didn't you?"

"The only thing I get out of Linked-in is the opportunity to congratulate other people on their new jobs."

"What you said and how you said it," Denise said, giving me a high five with her latex-gloved hand. "It's who you know and right now we don't know anybody."

"Well," I said as I turned to go back to my lab, "That's all about to change."

I was going straight to Jasmine's office; she's the manager of the Research Core Facility. She's about ten years older than me, married with kids, but we hang out sometimes. She's a newshound who keeps up on current events, watches CNN, and surfs the MSN.com website every hour on the hour.

"Hey, Jasmine," I said as I walked in the door and sat in the chair by her desk, "I need to get in the loop and I need to get in now."

"Preach, Tia, I feel you on that, I need to get in the loop myself," she said, leaning back in her chair. "I'm getting tired of being on the outside looking in the window at how the other half lives."

"I just need a game plan," I said, feeling excited. "My birthday is in two weeks on April 11th and I need to get some things working."

"It just so happens that I've got your first play; they're having an evening of networking at my church on Thursday so we can start there. I'm open to a higher career move and there might even be some eligible men in attendance."

"Jasmine, you are married. Why are you always looking for single men?" I asked.

"Child, I'm looking for you since you aren't making any progress. By the way I met this nice looking guy walking in Centennial Park the other day and he was really nice. He gave me his card if you want to call him. He's a teacher, divorced, and loves to cook, especially Bar-B-Q. He told me that he coaches middle school kids in track and field. Now, one thing, he had a big belly on him, but he was walking so that should not be a problem," she said proudly as if she had made some great discovery.

"How old is he, Jazz?" I asked.

"He told me he just turned 50."

"Uh-uh, I'm not going that old; I told you that I seriously don't want to go out with anybody over 40 years old."

"All right then," she said, cutting her eyes, "But if you want somebody with a job, who's going to call you by your God-given name instead of bitch, and knows how to treat a lady, you are going to have to raise that age limit."

"No, thanks," I said, shaking my head, "I'll keep looking."

"I hear you, Tia," she said with all the hand motions going, "But you need to get yourself an older man, be his tenderoni, and go on and live your life."

"No, girl, you are crazy, I got to have what I need in the bedroom," I reminded her.

"How do you know that an older man is not going to give you all you can handle in the bedroom?" she asked.

"I'm through with you, Jasmine," I said, standing up and

heading for the door, "I've got to get some work done today."

Why I haven't gotten married by now is puzzling to me. I've always had a boyfriend since I was old enough to know how to spell the word. I met Tim, my first serious boyfriend, when I started the 10th grade. He was my high school sweetheart. I don't know what I saw in him, he wasn't cute, belonged to a gang on the other side of the tracks, and sold drugs, but he was crazy about me. He didn't have a car and I thought it was sweet that he would walk so far to spend time with me. He never had money to take me places but it didn't matter because my mama would never let me go anywhere with him.

I didn't know it at the time but when we were in our senior year he got a fifteen year old freshman at another school pregnant. We were still together when I went to TSU and he even came to visit me at homecoming, but Tim worked at the same factory where my mama worked and when she saw him come to work with a hickey on his neck she wasted no time in telling me and by the end of the fall semester we were broken up.

I met my next boyfriend, Charles, while I was still with Tim. I wasn't looking for a relationship and he definitely wasn't my type. He was six-foot-six, light skin and light eyes, with a high top fade, and a thick heavy southern drawl. Charles was an electrical engineering major and he followed me around like a dog in heat. I wasn't interested in him, not even a little bit; I just got off on the attention he gave me. He's happily married now and he even named his baby after me. Thinking back, he was really nice looking and he turned out to be a good guy, but at the time I just wasn't attracted to him.

Most of my close friends in undergrad were male. There are three that I'm still close with and talk to on the regular. One is divorced, one single, and Freddy, who I was closest to back in the day, and who I thought was suspect at the time, is even married. I have to file that one as a missed prospect.

"Good morning, Dr. Lee," I said, walking into his office.

He was seated at his desk staring at his computer before he swiveled around to face me wearing a seldom seen smile. He was short and self-conscious about his stature; if you were standing he would prefer to stay seated. Although, his favorite stance was talking down at me while I was the one seated. Through his thick glasses I couldn't tell if his eyes were open or shut.

"Morning, Tia, I have good news for you," he said with his finger tips touching, "Your manuscript has been accepted in *The Cell* Journal. Therefore, your days here are numbered."

"Really, that is good news, Dr. Lee," I said out loud while my inner voice shouted, "It's about frigging time." I had been here for seven long years and now I was a short-timer.

"Now all I need for you to do is spend your time writing your dissertation and looking for your post-doctorate position because you're wasting my time," he said with no trace of the momentary grin he had worn, and then he turned his attention back to his computer.

I don't know why that man has always got to be so rude and disagreeable but he is not going to worry me today. I am so pumped that I am finally going to join Weight Watchers. I have been thinking about it, but today I'm so inspired that I'm going to do it. If it can work for Jennifer Hudson it can work for me. I sashay down the hall to my office and find the link on my laptop and from what I can tell from the description of the point system it gives me enough options to eat all day and not feel hungry. I'm not sure how that will lead to any weight loss but I'm down for not being hungry.

***

A few days later, it's Thursday and I'm still excited. Today is the professional networking reception at Jasmine's church and it's the first event in my new campaign. I decided to wear slacks and a knot blouse that drapes. Despite the fact that I'm a fashionista, my feet rarely let me strut my stuff in high heels and I hate wearing dresses with flats. I check my watch and skip dinner; I'm supposed to meet Jasmine at her house around 6:00 since the starting time is six-thirty.

"I ordered a pizza for Traci," Jasmine said when she answered the door, "Get you some while I get finished changing."

Traci was Jasmine's thirteen-year-old daughter. She was a cool kid, but she never had more than two words for me. The pizza smelled so good when I walked into the kitchen and I was starving, I hoped Traci wouldn't mind me sharing.

"Hey, Traci," I said, peeping my head in their den before I grabbed a plate.

"Hello," she answered, disinterested and never turning her head from the TV in my direction.

The pizza looked delicious, one slice wouldn't hurt my diet; I still had two points left from lunch.

"I don't know what the appropriate outfit for a networking mixer at a church is so I put on some dress pants and a dress shirt like yours," Jasmine said when she came down the stairs, "I guess we shouldn't be too formal."

"We look good," I said, "Business casual and ready to flow right into happy-hour."

"All right then, let's do this," she said, grabbing her handbag and keys and we both twisted out of the door and jumped in the car.

"Uh-uh, this is not looking good," I said when we arrived at the church and saw the parking lot was practically empty.

"This might be a let-down," Jasmine conceded, "But since we're here we might as well go in."

When we got inside the lobby there was a registration desk set up in the center so we went over to sign in.

"The registration fee is $10.00," the woman sitting at the table said after we signed our names.

"Never mind, Jazz, I don't have $10.00," I said, backing away from the table.

"Don't worry about it, I got you," Jasmine said as she dropped a twenty dollar bill on the table and pulled my arm towards the door of the gym area.

Then there was the second disappointment. There weren't a large number of booths exhibiting and none of them were promising opportunities for me.

"Let's make the most of it, girl," Jasmine said, pushing forward. "I don't think we're going to find a job in here but maybe we might find you a man. Let's get to networking."

We decided to visit every table and booth since we'd paid the twenty dollar fee. The first table belonged to Sprint and there was one nice-looking guy standing there. Jasmine went over and started a conversation with him about the jobs at the cell phone company.

Barely one minute had gone by before she asked, "I don't see a ring on your finger, are you married?"

I thought I was going to die.

"No, I'm not," he said with a chuckle.

"Are you involved?" she asked.

"Yes, I am," he said, still amused.

"Oh, that's too bad," Jasmine said, "Maybe you can tell us the spots in town where young single employed men like yourself who may not be spoken for hang out?"

He laughed again and said, "I'm sorry to say that I can't help you with that."

"Well thanks for your info about Sprint," she said, sounding dissatisfied, and then we moved on.

"What's wrong with your gaydar?" I asked her.

"What?" she replied, absolutely clueless.

"He was gay," I told her as we moved to the next booth.

"Oops, sorry, who knew? He was fine though and the brother was dressed to the 'T.'"

The next few tables we visited were represented by women. They were looking for counselors for the school system, customer service representatives, and volunteers to raise funds for charitable organizations. It was turning out to be a complete waste of time and then Jasmine zeroed in on a guy in a uniform looking for Army recruits.

"Don't do it, please," I begged, trying to stop her, but she was already in action asking him if he was married and where the spots were where single military men hung out.

He humored her and told us we had standing invitations at Fort Campbell in Clarksville, TN.

"If you want to know something you have to ask," she said, "We know not because we ask not."

We had gone around the room and there was only one vendor table left. Sitting there was an older guy dressed in a police uniform who looked like he had to be closing in on retirement.

Jasmine looked at me with a smile and said, "We might as well," and walked over to the table.

"We're not interested in becoming police women, but I was wondering if there are any handsome single policemen on the force?"

"Of course we have a few," he said, smiling.

"And where might we meet these gentlemen?" Jasmine asked.

"We have several social activities that we put on during the year."

"Really," said Jasmine, "How to we get invited to those?"

"I'll give you my e-mail and number and you can contact me and I'll let you know when we have our next party," he replied as he wrote his e-mail on the back of his card.

"Thank you, officer," Jasmine said, and we were finally out of the door.

I was never so happy to get out of one place in my life. I laughed about it with Jasmine in the car but to me it wasn't funny, it was downright disheartening. I dropped Jasmine off at her house around the corner and headed home. This was not the start I had hoped for. My plan definitely had to be tweaked or I was destined for failure.

2

Chapter Two

Yesterday's networking event was a complete wash. There wasn't a single job prospect, a single male prospect, and when I got home I didn't write a single word. I'm not about to let it bother me, this morning I am coming out fresh for round two.

"I have not yet begun to fight," I declared, staring at my reflection in the steamed-up mirror after my fifteen minute shower. I know I'm sexy but the hard truth is that I need to lose about 100 pounds. My Weight Watcher program truly has its work cut out for it. Anyway, the journey of a thousand miles begins with one step, so that's what I'm going to do, start walking. Centennial Park has a one mile loop and right after I leave the lab today I'm going to pound the pavement down and burn some calories.

Feeling charged up, I put on a skirt, a low cut blouse, some dangling earrings, and a bolero jacket to wear to the lab. Sometimes you need to show the world what you're working with. I rub some shea butter on my legs and slide my feet into some kitten heels. Looking this cute has me feeling more motivated by the minute. "I'm bad, I'm bad, and you know it," I tell the mirror after one last glance. I grab a banana on my way out of the door and that is zero points, so I'm already ahead for the day.

When I passed Dr. Lee in the hallway he couldn't even upset me with his usual negativity when he spouted off, "Have you written anything worth reading yet?"

"Forget him," I said calmly.

My writing is going well and I'm not going to let him get into my head and block my flow. I'm determined to graduate this semester and nothing will distract my focus on what I've got to do. I turn the corner and see Curtis Jefferson walking towards me. Now I've been crushing on this guy since we were first year students. He is one tall mug of hot cappuccino and I do need a pick me up.

"Hey you," I said as I opened up my arms and reached out for a hug. If I couldn't have it why couldn't I just hold it for a moment every now and then?

"That's a nice hello," he said, giving me a gentle squeeze.

"What's going on?" I asked him as we stepped back from the hug.

"Not much," he said, "More of the same."

"Same here," I said, walking away with a smile.

Now that was the way to get the day started I thought as the warmth of his body faded away from mine. Sitting in front of my laptop I wanted to take a few more minutes and imagine how I would have liked it to end, but I had a lot to do.

I spent the bulk of the day in my office trying to organize my data, create tables and diagrams for my results, and work on my introduction. I took a break after around 2:00 and microwaved a frozen meal I had in the office refrigerator for my lunch and before I knew it the rest of the day had flown by. I packed up my laptop and headed out to the parking lot pleased with my progress. My stomach was growling like a hungry bear but I was committed to exercising.

It was still a little chilly in the evenings despite the fact it was almost April. I stopped by my apartment and changed into my red Calvin Klein velour jogging outfit for my walk in the park. Why shouldn't I be stylish while in the process? I pulled into the park at the entrance near the pond and when I stepped out of the car I could hear music playing. That should get me moving to a good pace I thought.

The music was from the 80s, some Kashif and some Chic, so I was cool with it as I bounced to the beat in my brand new Skecher shape-ups I'd bought a few months back. After about ten minutes of walking I realized that this exercise thing was going to be a lot harder than I thought. I was out of breath, already sweating up my velour, and my feet were starting to ache. I now realized that my goal of walking for an hour might have been a bit ambitious to begin with. As I rounded the corner nearing the three-fourths of a mile marker I could see the three guys who where jamming and dee-jaying on a stage in the park.

When I had walked just a few feet past the edge of the stage, the one on the mic hollered out, "Hey Kool-aid."

Was he talking to me? I wasn't sure so I tried to play it off, looking ahead and picking up my pace.

Then he yelled again, "Hey Kool-aid."

I turned around slightly and he said, "Yeah you."

I sniggled, waved, and kept walking. Then I started thinking, did he mean I looked like the Mr. Kool-aid character from the commercial? I was about to start tripping and then I stopped myself. I'm not going to rush to judgment and take offense, even if he was referring to me as the Kool-aid man. I must be looking sweet and refreshing.

I pushed myself to keep walking and the second time I came around the stage the guy on the mic yelled, "Hey, hey, hey, Kool-aid."

That was over the top. It was definitely reminiscent of Fat Albert from the Cosby Kids. I kept my eyes facing forward thinking he better be glad that I'm tired or I might walk over there and battle him with my own rap.

"Keep calling me Kool-aid and you're gonna need a band-aid," I said under my breath.

Its lame I know, but hey I'm exhausted. It would take the last ounce of my strength to get to my car and I had worked up an appetite. They would get a pass today.

***

The week sped by in a blur and I needed to drive to Pulaski to check on my mama. My parents had moved there about ten years ago when my daddy's job at the Gabriel factory was relocated. Going to visit them there was not one of my favorite things to do. The town was as country as you could get and it was like driving back to Mayberry RFD. All that's left is for Andy Griffith and Barney Fife to pull me over and give me a ticket.

It's only seventy-five miles away but I really don't feel like driving, I've been on the road every other weekend for the last month. My mama has diabetes and her doctors believe that she also has early onset Alzheimer's to go with it. She keeps refusing to go back to the doctor for her appointments so I have to keep a close eye on her.

I love my mama even though she's hard-headed. She and Daddy have a strange relationship. They get along very well but it's more like roommates. The lovey-dovey part between them has been over for a long time. My suspicions, from the snide remarks she makes about him from time to time, are that he committed some transgression with another woman back in his younger years that she is not about to forgive him for it in this lifetime. As far as I'm concerned my daddy is a good man and has been good to her for as long as I can remember, and she's not easy to live with. I think that whatever happened she should have let it go by now.

About ten miles from home I notice a black Chrysler 300 behind me.

"What is up with this?" I asked, looking in my rearview mirror.

They are entirely too close on my tail. Uh- uh, now he is driving right beside my car door. My eyes dart down to look at the speedometer and we are both driving over seventy miles an hour.

"What's your problem?" I mouthed through the window glass, pressing down harder on the gas.

I pull ahead but the car speeds up and is beside me again. I take another look out and through the tinted glass I can see it's a brother flashing me a grin while he's rolling down his window.

"Hey girl, can I get that number?" he yelled from his window.

My number, is this fool crazy? We are on the interstate driving seventy miles an hour and he's trying to carry on a conversation.

"Pull over," he said, motioning with his hands.

What's really truly crazy and I can't believe it, is that I was actually doing it. I pulled off on the shoulder and he stopped not far behind me. I use my side mirror to watch him as he steps out of his car and I can see that he is tall with a slim build. His hands are visible and empty so I think I'm safe. He comes over to my car door and bends down to speak to me through the half-rolled-down window.

"So, what's your name, shorty?" he asked me.

"For real, you chased me down to ask me my name," I said dumbfounded.

"Yes I did. You look real good to me," he said, nodding his head in approval. "Where are you headed?"

"Tia, and I'm on my way to Pulaski," I said, "Who are you and what are you doing running people down on the interstate?"

Then the brother proceeds to tell me, "I'm Marcus, and I'm going to make you my woman."

This I've got to see I think to myself before I said, "I'm a perfect stranger that you saw pass you in a car and you see a relationship out of that."

"I'd like to take you out to dinner and a movie," he said, ignoring my response. "I'm about to check into a hotel here. Call me, and we'll hook up later," he said, writing his cell number on a piece of paper and then handing it to me.

I kept him in view through the side mirror as he strolled back to his car confident as hell. I tossed the number on the seat and pulled off so fast I skid my tires. I refused to look anywhere but straight ahead all the way home.

"Mama, it's me," I shouted, coming in the side door off the kitchen.

"I'm in the living room," she hollered back.

I knew where she was without her saying a word. My mama was as much a permanent fixture in the living room in front of the TV as the coffee table.

"How are you feeling?" I asked, patting her on the shoulder.

"I'm fine I keep telling y'all," she answered, "It's all of you who are worrying me to death."

"I love you too, Mama. Where's Daddy?" I asked, sitting down beside her on the sofa.

"At work, at least that's what he told me," she replied.

"Have you eaten?"

"Yeah, he made me something before he left."

I sat there watching Wheel of Fortune for a few minutes and then I took my overnight bag to my room to unpack. My laptop beckoned me to get some work done but I looked away. I wasn't in the mood for writing. Before I could give it a second thought, I picked up my cell phone, pulled the slip of paper out of my pocket, and called the guy from the interstate. Why, I don't know, curiosity, or maybe just boredom.

"What's up?" Marcus said answering.

"It's Tia, you ran me off the road earlier."

"I been waiting for you to call, there's a restaurant near here, won't you come meet me and we can get to know each other."

"I'll be there in twenty minutes," I said, surprising myself before I hung up.

I brushed my teeth, ran a comb through my hair, and put on some lip gloss.

"I'll be back, Mama, I'm going to meet a friend and get something to eat," I shouted towards the living room before I went out of the side door and drove the three miles to the restaurant.

In less than five minutes I walked into IHOP and saw him sitting at a table near the back, but before I could get there and sit down he smiled wide, and those two gold teeth shining like head lights in the front of his mouth said all there was to be said.

"Hello beautiful, I'm glad you made it," he said, without standing up or pulling out my chair.

"Why did I stop?" I asked myself.

This guy is probably a drug dealer. I must have been in a daze or hypnotized by the white line on the road. But I was here and hungry so I sat down at the table.

"Get whatever you want," he said, nodding his head.

"The sky is the limit," I said mockingly, picking up the thin menu.

"You got that right," he said staring at me.

I kept my eyes on the menu even though I knew it by heart. The waitress came over and took our order and when she walked away he found his sexy voice and said, "I wanna be with you."

"No, Marcus," I said, "It's not like that, I don't know you."

"You won't be disappointed," he said, looking at me with narrowed eyes.

"You have got me mixed up, I'm here trying to get to know you," I repeated to him.

"Now you tripping, you can get to know me later. I wanna be

with you."

"No, I don't get down like that," I said, insulted, "I need to know you first."

"All right, I can respect that, but my birthday is on May 2nd, if you're not going to be with me, I'm going to be celebrating it with somebody else."

For real! What is this man talking about, I don't even know him. One thing I'm sure of is that one of us is real crazy, and since I'm still sitting here it might be me.

He just kept talking, "You don't appreciate me and what I can do for you. I can take care of you; get you off that job that you don't like. I'm talking about taking you to a dealership tomorrow and buying you a car."

"It's not about money for me," I said, "Where do you work anyway?"

"I work at the Purdue chicken plant."

Okay, now I'm done. This was not some fantasy of meeting the man of my dreams by chance on the interstate; this had turned into a nightmare. I finished my meal, told him I would call him when I got back to Nashville, then we would hook up, not.

When I got back to my mama's house, I went straight into the living room and told her about the guy I met at seventy miles an hour and then what happened at our dinner.

"Tia, I didn't know you were so desperate that you would even talk to some nut flagging you down on the interstate. What is wrong with you?" Mama asked with her face all frowned up.

I didn't have an answer so I called it a night and went to my room. "What was wrong with me, was I that desperate?"

I wondered, lying awake in my bed. Maybe she was right. I thought I was just being curious. Okay maybe I'm a little anxious and that proves to be very dangerous in making good decisions. I decided to concentrate on finishing my terminal degree, getting myself established, and leaving the men alone for a while.

"What are the errands you needed me to run for you, Mama?" I asked her the next morning after breakfast.

"Do you think you can handle them without getting sidetracked," she asked, making a joke. "Last night you ran out of here barely saying hello."

"Come on, Mama, I have learned my lesson on that one. I shouldn't have even told you about it. Now, what do you need me to do?"

"Shoot, I can't even think right now, you got my mind confused with your foolishness, but I need some things from the grocery store."

"Do you have a list made?" I asked patiently.

"I think I need some milk and butter," she answered absentmindedly.

I looked in the refrigerator and there was a nearly full gallon of milk and a pound of low-sodium butter on the top shelf. Most of the time she was fine, but her memory was fading out more and more. My daddy couldn't stand it so he worked all the hours they would give him and was hardly around except to sleep. My heart sank when I thought about the day when she wouldn't know who I was. I looked through the shelves and drawers and in the pantry and made a list of whatever things I thought were needed.

The rest of the weekend flew by with my nieces and nephews coming by wanting all of my attention, and me trying to read my mother's fleeting thoughts. When it was time to go I hadn't written one word. On the drive back to Nashville I pumped up the volume on the radio and kept my eyes looking straight ahead.

***

Monday morning had come too quickly once again. Two days off just aren't enough.

"I'm ready for your introduction and your literature review," Dr. Lee said to me as I pretended not to see him when he passed me on the way to my office.

I turned on my computer to write and I sat there so long without typing a word that my screen saver came on. I was watching the lines of peppermint candy moving up and across and down and diagonal on the screen in amazement when this tall hunk of dark chocolate dressed in Dockers and a Polo shirt appeared in the doorway. This was a wake-up call if I ever saw one.

"Excuse me," he said, "I'm Reggie Woods, a representative from Phenix Scientific. Would you mind telling me where your lab buys it disposable plastics?"

"Hello, I'm Tia, a soon to be graduating student," I said, reaching out my hand. "It's a pleasure to meet you."

Unfortunately, we bought so much stuff in bulk that I was sure he wasn't going to make a sale in Dr. Lee's lab, but I didn't want to let him get away that quickly. I wanted to find out more about him but I didn't want to come across as the desperate person that my mama seemed to think I was. I knew

Jasmine could get all the info I needed to know without me having to say a word.

"I'll take you to our Research Core Facility; a lot of the supplies we use are ordered through them," I said.

I stood up to lead the way and it was all I could do to keep from taking his hand or putting my arm around him. I tried to do my slow roll sexy walk just ahead of him, again, it never hurts to show them what you working with. Today, with him trailing behind me, it felt like a long walk around the corner and down the hall. Jasmine's door is always open. When we walked in I could see the light flash in her eyes when she turned from her desk and saw us. She must not have an off switch because she's always on and ready.

"Hello, hello, Tia, who is this nice gentleman you have with you today?" she asked, her eyebrows rising with interest.

"This is Reggie, he's a salesperson from Phenix Scientific making his rounds."

"Glad to meet you, Reggie, we don't get many interesting black male salespeople coming to see us," Jasmine said, standing up and shaking his hand with a smile before she got to work on her investigative report. "Do you work out of Nashville or are you from out of town?"

"Nashville is within my region, but I live in Atlanta," he replied.

"Atlanta, that's not too far, what kinds of things do you like to do for fun in Atlanta?"

"My father has a farm on the outside of town with a few horses. Do you like to ride?"

"I haven't had the opportunity to ride one except for the pony at the zoo when I was a lot younger. They led it around in a circle by a rope. Does that count?"

"No, it doesn't," he said, chuckling. "Let me know if you're ever in the city and you can come by for a ride."

"We'd love that wouldn't we, Tia?" she said, looking at me like we hit the jackpot.

"What else do you like to do for fun in Atlanta?" she asked, sitting down and scooting her chair closer.

"I like to sing," he answered with a big smile.

"Oh you do," she exclaimed, as if he'd said he was Superman and could leap tall buildings in a single bound.

"Would you like me to sing something for you?" he asked, totally confident.

"Absolutely," she answered, excited and already clapping her hands.

"Who's your favorite singer?"

"Luther Vandross of course," she replied, "But I like a lot of male singers."

"I sing a lot of Sam Cooke, choose any song except *Change gon come*."

"Okay," Jasmine said, thinking for a moment, "What about, *You send me?*"

This Negro, and I use the word affectionately, opened up his mouth and started to sing and I don't know much Sam Cooke music, but I do know when an angel starts to sing. Ooh, he sounded so sweet and clear and he sent me, yes he did. I didn't know where I was going, yes it was infatuation, and I found myself wanting to marry him. I covered my mouth with my hand and I think I felt a tear in my eye. When he finished

Jasmine started to clap her hands again.

"That was so good," she said, "You can really sing. Now, are you married?"

He hesitated for a minute and we held our breath waiting for his answer.

"It's a long story," he said.

"Well, I've got time and this campus has eligible women who want to know," Jasmine said anxiously.

"I'm separated and in the process of getting a divorce and I have two children that we're fighting over for shared custody."

"Wow, that's deep," she said, feeling his pain, "Sometimes things don't work out."

"Tell me about it," he said. "Anyway, I got my rounds to finish. How about I come back by when I'm done and you two show me where I can get some good Nashville barbeque?"

"Sure we can," Jasmine said, "You know where to find us after you handle you business."

"I certainly do," he said, smiling.

We both watched him as he walked out.

"Girl, what in the world is wrong with you? That's your man right there in front of your face and you had nothing to say. You need some of that in your life," Jasmine said, pointing in his direction.

"He's married," I told her, feeling let-down. "Damn, he could sing too. I love a man who can sing. Plus he was my type, dark, husky, and a little rugged looking. Why does this always happen to me?"

"The man said he's separated and getting a divorce," Jasmine reminded me.

"You can't believe them when they say that, don't you ever take off those rose colored glasses?" I asked, exasperated.

"Why should I?" she protested. "I like my rose colored glasses. I'm going to take the man at his word unless he gives me a reason not to. You better get on that, Tia, and stop talking about how you can't find anybody. That man walked into your office and already you're second guessing it after only fifteen minutes. Go on out to lunch and get to know some more about the man before we cross him off the list."

"What have I got to lose," I thought, walking back down the hall, at least I'll get a free lunch out of it.

Reggie came back by the lab around 12:30, knocking on the inside of the door. "I'm taking my lunch break, are you ready to get some food?"

"I would settle for just getting out and getting some air right now," I told him, shutting down my computer. "I'm trying to write and it's going slow. Let's go by and get Jasmine."

"We're ready to go, Jasmine" I announced when we walked into her office.

"You two are going to have to go without me, I can't get away right now, but you two can bring me something back," Jasmine said, pulling a fast one.

It was just her ploy of sending us out by ourselves so we could talk. I gave her a knowing look before Reggie and I left. I gave him directions and we headed over to Jack's Bar-B-Que. He parked, hurried out and opened the car door for me, earning some gentleman points.

In the food line he said, "Order something good, I'll have whatever you're having, and don't forget Jasmine."

"The ribs are delicious but I probably should stick with the chicken, I'm trying to lose some weight," I said, adding up the weight watcher points in my head.

"If you want the ribs, get them, I like a woman with some meat on her bones," he said, smiling down at me.

He was speaking my language and I definitely didn't have a problem with that. He paid the tab and we sat down to eat. We had a good time. He talked a lot, mostly about himself, but it was kind of cute.

"May I have your number?" he asked politely when we got back to the research building. "I'd like to keep in touch and call you when I get back in town."

"I don't see why not," I said, looking him in the eyes.

"That's what's up," he said, smiling again.

We exchanged cell phone numbers and I wanted to really see if he's for real, but I'm not interested in a long distance relationship. I've tried them before and in my opinion they don't work, mainly because this girl's gotta have it on the regular, despite the fact that I haven't had any for months. Furthermore, I don't have time to worry about him right now anyway, it's halfway through April and I still have half of my dissertation to write. Not only that, Yvonne's wedding is next month.

"How was lunch?" Jasmine asked when I dropped her food off in the lab.

"Forget about him, and I don't want to talk about it," I said, frustrated that there was always a hitch whenever I met a fine brother I was interested in.

"Talk to him, Tia, you never know. You don't have anything to lose."

3

Chapter Three

Reggie and I have been texting back and forth over the last week and it's been pretty cool. I haven't had time to call him and have a real conversation because I've been writing my ass off. I've finally got my momentum going and my dissertation is taking shape. I'm almost sure that the light at the end of the tunnel is not a gorilla with a flashlight.

"I need that first draft, Tia, you need to hurry up," Dr. Lee had the nerve to tell me as soon as I walked in on Friday, "I'll probably have to write it all over again myself anyway."

I hate him and the devil is a liar. He's the one who can't speak or write in proper English, and just to be on the safe side I'm going to let Jasmine edit it for me before I give it to him. It's got to be submitted to my committee in less than two weeks if I'm going to graduate and march in May. I'm running out of time and I haven't even begun to look for a post-doc position. All this pressure and anxiety is getting me hungry. What's more, I used up all of my breakfast points and half of my lunch points on a bacon and egg sandwich this morning.

I'm stressing over getting my references in endnote and I can tell it's time for a break. I need a pick-me-up and I know just where to find it. I take the short walk to Curtis's lab.

"Hey, how's the writing going," he said, loading his samples in a protein gel.

"It's coming slowly," I said, moving in closer for the kill. "I need a hug."

I put my arms around him and squeezed him close to my breast and had to fight a tough battle against my urges before I could let him go. That felt mmm, mmm, good, just what this future doctor ordered. His lab mate, Josiah, came in as I was leaving, he was such a dog and not my type. He looked down into my cleavage and licked his lips.

"Where's my hug?" he said, grabbing me and pressing himself up against all my goodies, top and bottom shelf.

"Bye, Josiah," I said after I peeled his body off of mine and walked out. I guess you have to take the good with the bad.

I wrote for about another hour and I started to feel starved, not just for food but for real male companionship. That momentary hug just didn't do it for me. I need a man of my own on call or either waiting at the house when I get there, deprivation just isn't my thing. I packed up my data, clicked off my laptop, and went down the hall to see if Denise wanted to hang out tonight, it was time to throw out a net and see what I could catch.

"Hey, D, what's up for this evening? I feel like hanging out tonight."

"Not tonight, girlfriend, I'm kicking it with Andre as soon as I get off. He's missed a couple of nightshifts and it's time for him to get on the job."

"I feel you on that, except I need to get somebody employed in that position."

"I know you, Tia, you've got a number tucked away

somewhere to fill in as a temporary."

"I wish I did, D, have a good weekend," I said on the way out of her lab.

Denise didn't understand that things had changed a lot since undergrad. Guys circulated around us like flies at a picnic back then, nowadays a hot prospect was a rare bird. I made a right turn to Jasmine's office, hoping I wouldn't have to go on the hunt by myself.

"Come on, Jazz, we going out on the prowl tonight," I said to Jasmine at her office door, "We have got to get in the loop and I need to meet a man. I hear there is a really nice happy-hour at this new place off 12th Avenue North, Benton House of Blues."

"Nothing but a word, girl, I'm ready whenever," Jasmine said eagerly.

I think she's getting restless too. She says her husband has been tripping lately, working a ton of hours and ignoring her, but that woman doesn't know how lucky she is.

"That's a bet, we'll ride in my car and go over there after work," I said, going back to collect my things.

On the short drive over to Benton's I was starting to feel good. I hadn't been out in so long. A woman needs the attention that she gets in a night spot sometimes, especially if she's not getting any at home, and that applies to the single and the married, the young and the old. We all gotta have it. Except, when we got to the club, it was déjà vu, the parking lot was virtually empty.

"Oh no, not this again," Jasmine said and threw up her hands.

"Just wait a minute before you go off, it's still early, the party crowd hasn't gotten here yet," I said, trying to stay optimistic for her sake as well as my own.

"Okay, let me chill for a minute," she said, taking a deep breath with her hand on her chest.

Jasmine is so dramatic. Even so, when we walked in the door it got worse. There were about twelve people inside. We had our choice of tables so we chose one in the middle, sat down, and took another look around.

"Girl, it's nothing but the usual in here," I said with a sigh. "There's the one that looks like he's too old to be hanging out in any club, there's the one that looks like he just got off of a very dirty job and didn't go home to get cleaned up or change clothes, over there a table of four who look a little too young and too ghetto to be here, and last but not least there's a couple of guys who look like they've already made a love connection with each other."

"Yep, that's about the size of it," Jasmine agreed, "No hopes of anybody buying us a drink in here and they're buy-one-get-one-free. Anyway, I'm thirsty, do you want one?"

"You know I don't drink, Jazz."

"That may be the reason for some of your problems," she said, laughing.

A minute later she comes back with two cokes and said, "I usually make it a point not to frequent places that serve drinks in cheap plastic cups that I can't see through."

"Shut up," I told her, holding in my laugh.

We sat there for about a half hour not believing it was as bad as it was. I could tell Jasmine was getting impatient and ready to go but I wanted to give it some time to jump off, after all its Friday. Then I see a guy who I went to undergrad with walk in with a friend and I raise up in my chair to get his attention. He nods in recognition as he goes over to the bar to get a drink. The two of them walk over to our table with beers in both their hands and join us, and of course they don't offer us anything.

"Hey, Tia, what's up?" he said, and then introduced his friend, "This is Doug."

We spend a few minutes catching up. He's working at Dupont making that long money and it gives me some hope on the job front but I notice a twang in his voice that hadn't always been there. We run out of conversation quickly and exchange numbers in our phones and then they move to another table closer to the empty stage.

"It looks like it's an epidemic in the city to me, honey, the only couples in here are gay. What's really going on?" Jasmine asked.

I give up hope after another half hour and drive her back to her car. My phone rings before I can pull off and I think its Jasmine calling to wear me out some more about the dud happy-hour.

"Hey, Tia, what's up with you?" Yvonne said, complaining. "Do you ever read your emails? Do you know how hard it is to pull a wedding together in two months? It's getting close and you have not even come up here for your fitting."

"I have been pressed trying to write my paper so I can graduate" I said, attempting to bring her out of her selfish mode. "I've got a lot going on here."

My defense fell on deaf ears; she kept fussing, "I don't have time to wait for you to get up here. I'm going to have to replace you as a bridesmaid, but I need you to be a hostess. Make sure you have a violet colored dress. I'll talk to you later." Then she hung up before I could say anything.

I had barely driven a block when the phone rang again. "What is it now, Yvonne?" I thought when I said hello and pushed speaker phone so I could drive.

"Hey, Tia, I called to tell you your mama is not doing too good," my daddy said, "She's forgetting to take her medicine and she's swelling all over. She's being hardheaded and won't let me take her to the doctor."

"I'm on my way, Daddy," was all I could say.

I really don't need this now, Dr. Lee is pressing my ass against the wall and I've got to get back to my writing, but that's my mama so I've got to go home. I find the nearest gas station, swipe my credit card to fill up my car, and get on interstate 65 heading south. I walked in the door in less than 80 minutes.

"Mama, how are you feeling?" I asked, even though looking at her I knew it wasn't good.

"I'm fine, Tia, your daddy didn't need to call and worry you," she said, barely able to stand or walk, "I don't need to go see no doctor. I need to be left alone."

"Tell it to the man in the ambulance," I said, laying down the law and pushing 911 into my phone. I'm not listening to her mess for another minute.

I ride in the back of the ambulance with the EMT while Daddy trails us in his car. Thank God we don't have a long wait. I stand on the other side of the curtain while Mama is examined and my nerves are on end.

"We're going to admit Mrs. King," the attending physician

in the hospital emergency room tells us, "She's retained a large amount of fluid that can either be caused by her kidneys or heart, and her sugar is elevated. We need to run some tests before we can say anything definite."

"I've got to get to work, baby," Daddy says, giving me a kiss on the cheek before he leaves.

I'm sure Mama has run him ragged and he needs a break. The report from the doctor really has me worried because I can't be in two places at one time. It's time to call my brother, Thomas, she's his mama too. I can only stay around for a couple of days. I step out into the waiting room to call him.

"Thomas, the doctors are keeping Mama, they're not sure what's wrong yet."

"This really isn't a good time for Mama to be sick," he explains, "Me and my lady are having some serious problems right now, and we might split up."

"Bye, Thomas," I said, hanging up and wondering what all that even had to do with our Mama. I sat at the hospital for the rest of the weekend, and thankfully they got some of the fluid off and her sugar level lowered. They were going to release her in the morning which was good because I could only stay for one more day before Dr. Lee had another reason to ride my ass.

I got up early Tuesday morning and headed straight to the campus without eating breakfast. My life had gotten so chaotic that I didn't have the tolerance or willpower to keep counting Weight Watcher points so I drove to the Marathon gas station to get a big bacon and egg sandwich. Inside my office I said a short blessing over my food and prayed for a miracle to get me through this dissertation. I only had two days before I had to submit my final paper to my committee so they would have it two weeks before my final meeting and I didn't need hunger as a distraction.

I sent the introduction and literature review for Jasmine to edit while I got my figures and data in order. Dr. Lee stuck his head in my office to see if I was there working and I was glad I was present and accounted for, but his attitude was messing with my confidence. Here I was less than a month from completing my Ph.D. in Cell Biology and this man made me feel like I was as dumb as a door nail. I had every intention of wiping that superior look off his face with a completed manuscript in less than forty-eight hours.

"You have got to stop letting him get to you, girl, you are among the best and the brightest that this country has to offer. We may not get recognized and we might not get the big dollars, but we are accomplished individuals," Jasmine said, trying to get me geeked. "I'm going to have to play you my new 'old school' theme song."

She got on the computer and went to Youtube and played Curtis Mayfield's song, *'We're a winner.'* It was a little before my time but I got into it, it had a nice groove and the words did snap me out of my daze, "*Never let anybody say you can't make it cause a feeble mind is in your way.*" Tia King still reigns supreme.

***

"Good morning Dr. Lee," I said on Thursday, "Here is the hard copy of the final draft of my dissertation and I've e-mailed you a copy also."

"It's about time, Tia, you really pushed it to the limit," he said smugly.

"No matter," I replied, "It's right on time."

It feels like I'm walking on air when I leave his office and he doesn't make a snide remark. It's a done deal. I have submitted my paper to Dr. Lee and the rest of my committee members and I have a scheduled date for my defense. I only get one day to celebrate because my next battle is getting my power point together and standing in front of the opposing army and taking their direct hits.

I spent the rest of the morning and afternoon on the computer and my eyes were burning. I took my contacts out and put on my glasses, snatched up my purse, and called it a day. I stopped by the Research Core on my way out to check with Jasmine.

"It's time to take a blow," Jasmine said, "You have worked your ass off. You need to take this night and relax for a minute."

"Let's head down to Jazz and Jokes and get our laugh on," Denise said, popping her head in the door.

I didn't need much convincing. "Let's go," I cheered, happy to go out with my girls and relax on my twenty-four hour reprieve.

Jasmine drove downtown in her car and I sat in the back.

"At least my hair is done, because these are definitely not my night-on-the-town clothes," I said.

"You look good, child, don't worry about it," Jasmine said, pulling into the parking lot.

"The club is nice even though it's a little small inside," Denise commented after we sat down at a table near the stage.

"You've got to have a small drink to celebrate today," Jasmine said, ordering a round for all of us and some hot wings.

"Why not," I sighed, "I deserve to kick back and relax."

The food and wine comes, we do some eating and drinking, and I'm starting to feel Gucci. I've come a long way and I can finally see myself moving forward, a smile is sneaking around my lips, and then he walks in. It was Anthony Williams, the first man to truly break my heart. We made eye contact but he turned away like he never knew me or laid between my legs. I tried to follow suit and pretend I didn't know him either but I couldn't help looking over at his table. Jasmine with her in-tuned self sensed a different vibe in the air. "Do you know that guy who just walked in?" she asked.

"Yeah, he was one of my exes," I answered, hoping to sound indifferent.

"Girl you got more exes than Elizabeth Taylor," she said with a laugh.

"We used to live together," I told them, watching him out of the side of my eye.

"What?" Denise said shocked, "I didn't know you had ever lived with anybody."

They both turned and looked over at the table where Anthony sat with another woman, trying to make sense of what I just said.

"Why didn't he speak or say hello if you two were that tight?" Jasmine asked, taken aback.

"I thought he was the one," I murmured as my mind flashed back.

I met Tony at TSU when I was a freshman in the engineering department during the second semester. It started off as the best part of my life, I was surrounded by men all the time. We all

48

went to class together and ate together. I was in Chemistry lab one day when this dark-skinned brother with a hat on walked up and starting talking to me.

"What did you make on the physics test?" he asked boldly.

"Are you in my physics class too?" I asked him, wondering why I had never noticed him before. He was dark chocolate, just like I liked them.

"Yeah I am. You're usually talking to some other dude when your head is not deep in your books," he said.

"You're right," I said, laughing.

He told me his name was Tony and that he was from Ohio. After that we became friends and by the end of freshman year we were dating. We were a couple all through college visiting each other's family homes but nobody in my family liked him. My mother said he looked like a black duck. I knew he wasn't all that cute, but I loved him. We drifted apart some after graduation dating off and on. I don't know what it was about him that I loved so much, I just know I did.

It was lonely for me on the off times while I was working and coming home to an empty apartment. I really wanted somebody to share my life with. One night I was praying for the Lord to send me my husband and as soon as I said amen, the phone rang, and it was him. I just knew he was the one, it was the answer to my prayer. We started talking again and eventually we moved into a condo together for about a year until he started hanging out with this girl at his job. He told me that they were just friends but I suspected he was telling her the same thing about me. He came home late one night and I asked, "What's really going on?"

We started arguing and I stopped point blank and asked him, "Tony, when are we going to get married?"

"I love you, but not enough to marry you," he answered without hesitation.

"What game are we playing if this relationship is not going anywhere?" I asked, getting upset.

"It's not a game, I just can't see myself marrying you."

"Get out, I can't talk to you anymore or be your friend," I screamed, going off the deep end.

It used to make me cry when I would see him at church after we broke up. He still used to call me every now and then, and when another woman slashed his tires I replaced them for $300. He swore he would pay me back but he never did. I guess that's why he can't look me in the face. When I heard he got married it made me a little sad. I heard she was an older woman who's a doctor. I guess he succeeded in finding someone to take care of him. If I wasn't the proud and progressive sister that I am, I would go right over there and ask that Negro for my money.

I turned my attention back to the comedy on stage and vowed not to let my eyes roll over to their table for the rest of the night.

The comedian was an older guy but I had seen him do a set before on BET and he was pretty funny. I laughed at his jokes and let it all go. This was my time, my night, and I wasn't going to let my mood get sucked back into the past. We ordered another round of drinks and even the cold fries and wings hit the spot. We walked out of the club and the comedian was out front shaking hands and flirting with the ladies.

"I enjoyed the show," Jasmine told him.

He responded saying "Thank you, pretty lady."

He said something to Denise too but I couldn't hear what it was.

When he saw me he crossed his arms with a big smile on his face and said, "All right, here is the sexy librarian."

"Uh-uh," I said, "I don't believe he's clowning me like that."

Jasmine and Denise starting cracking up and Jasmine said, "It's because you're wearing your glasses, that church dress and sweater, and those flats.

I looked at my outfit and I got another laugh too, but I made a promise that this was going to be the last time I stepped out office casual going to a club.

I got good news on Monday; my committee didn't have any issues with my paper so I could focus on putting my power-point together and practice my presentation. I had less than two weeks to pull it all together. I also had to figure out what I was going to wear; I needed to be both professional and comfortable.

***

"You're ready, girl, remember you're a winner," Jasmine said after I went through my presentation for the second time on the night before my defense. "Take some deep breaths before you start, speak out to the audience, make a little eye contact, and keep a steady pace. Pause and take a sip of water if you start to feel rushed or get nervous and out of breath."

"I hope that a lot of people don't come, I'm already nervous," I said, turning off my computer, "I'll be so glad when this is over."

"Have you decided what you're wearing," Jasmine asked, "You don't want to wear anything tight that will make you self-conscious."

"Yes, I know what I'm wearing. I bought a new dress that has a jacket to match. I'm putting on flats though, I don't want my feet to hurt standing up there for an hour."

"Don't worry about it, you'll be fine," she assured me.

"I start shaking whenever I think about it."

"You going to have to calm down or you'll be a wreck, and then you won't give a good presentation," Jasmine said. "You need to take the edge off. I'm going to make you a water bottle with a shot of rum in it."

"No way, I'm not going to get up there and make a fool of myself."

"It's not enough to get you drunk, it will mellow you out."

"No, thank you," I told her, "I need all my senses together to get through this."

"Okay, I'll bring it in the morning just in case."

I barely slept that night. If I could get through the morning, I would be Dr. Tia King in the afternoon. I got up early and went over my power-point again before I showered. Then I started the long process of putting on my game face.

Inside the auditorium I paced back and forth while the students and faculty member drifted in as the time approached 10:00. Mama, Daddy, and my brother Thomas got there on time, thank God, and they took a seat near the front on the end. It hurt my heart to see Mama sitting in a wheel chair though. When I saw Jasmine walk in and take a seat I paced over to her row.

"Do you have it?" I asked with my hand held out, hoping.

"Yeah," she said, reaching down in her bag and handing me the spiked water bottle.

I stood at the side while Dr. Lee started my introduction.
I could feel everybody watching me as I moved towards the
podium to begin. I felt like they were all waiting for me to
make a mistake, especially Dr. Lee, so he would be justified for
the hard time he had given me. Suddenly, I wished I could dim
the lights lower because I felt like I was up there butt naked
without a wax. I took a long swig from the bottle and felt the
cool water that went down warm, flow through my body and
soothe my nerves.

I read the title of my dissertation and proceeded on through
my presentation. It was surreal; there were moments when I
felt like I was sitting in the audience watching myself. With
the help of a few sips of my tonic water I made it through, took
all the questions like a champ, and did my acknowledgements.
When I heard the applause I knew it was a done deal.

"Ladies and gentlemen, I have the pleasure of presenting to
you, Dr. Tia King," Dr. Lee said at my reception. "We are so
proud of her many accomplishments and the acceptance of
her manuscript into The Cell Journal. Join us in a toast to the
success of her future endeavors."

It was all I could do to maintain my control and put on one
of the same fake smiles he was wearing, this man had put
me through hell, and my first instinct was to take that plastic
champagne cup and jam it down his throat. Once again and
hopefully for the last time, I refused to give him the power to
ruin my day.

"Congratulations, Tia," Curtis said, giving me a hug in front
of the serving line.

"Thank you" I said, milking this dose of human kindness for

all it was worth, "I'm waiting for you to finish."

I held him as close as I could, wishing I could feel his skin against mine instead of these clothes. I had to let go before I caused a scene since there were others standing there who wanted to wish me well.

"You did it, girl," Jasmine said, giving me a hug, "You see there was nothing to worry about. It was a job well done."

"I needed that water though, it hit the spot," I said, raising my hand for a high five.

"By any means necessary," she said, slapping my hand and holding it.

I spent the afternoon receiving congratulations, hugs, and sharing horror stories with other students. We ate and drank, and then we cut the cake. My mama and daddy were so proud of me, they smiled the whole time. I was the center of attention. I almost felt like a bride. Except after all the celebrating, I woke up alone the morning after and there was no honeymoon. My family had gone back to Pulaski and I seriously had to find a job and make my next move.

"Look at who it is this morning, Hello Dr. King," Jasmine said when I showed up at her office the next day.

"Yeah, it's like I never left," I said with a smile, "I've got to print my dissertation on this heavyweight woven paper and submit it to the graduate school by tomorrow if I want to march in the graduation ceremony."

"I suppose you want to use my laser printer," Jasmine said, looking at the box of the special paper in my hand.

"You know I don't have any money for Kinko's."

"I'm just teasing you, I'm here for whatever you need. I still haven't recovered from the post-traumatic stress of my starving student days."

"Why haven't you gotten a better job since you got your Ph.D.?" I asked curiously, wondering why she hadn't moved on.

"I have been trying but it's not that easy. When people look at my CV they think that research is all I can do even though I have a degree in higher education administration."

"Have you been applying for positions here?"

"Whenever I come across one, I apply, but I've only had two interviews."

"That's crazy," I told her, loading my paper into the printer.

"I don't want to be a killjoy or scare you but the job market in this economy is nothing to write home about. It's tough."

"I don't need anything else to worry about; I just got out of the fire," I said, not wanting to lose the afterglow of my defense.

"Now you're going into the frying pan, Tia. I was so excited when I graduated with my doctorate. I went to Brooks Brothers and bought myself a gray pinstripe suit and one of their tailored shirts to match. I wanted to be confident and sharp when I scheduled all of my interviews. When I got a call for the first one I was ready, you should have seen me."

"Girl, you are so dramatic. How much did that suit cost you?" I asked

"I can't tell you, you couldn't take it right now. Just know I was shit sharp, my hair was French-rolled, my make-up was understated, and I was pure professional. I strolled into my appointment right at the top of the hour. "Hello Dr. Green," the woman interviewing me said, "I hope you won't mind if the members you will be working with sit in on the interview." Not at all, I answered politely, sitting at the head of the conference room table looking like the picture of success. The woman looked me in my face and then at my well-fitting suit and then she smiled. "This position only pays $41 thousand and I don't know if that would interest you," she said to me with a questioning look. I told her that it wasn't the money that interested me; I was wanting to transition out of lab research and into administration and this job would help me to accomplish that. We went through the motions of the interview but I knew the sight of me in my new suit had killed any chances I had of getting that job."

"They should have given you the choice," I remarked while my paper continued to churn and pile up on the printer.

"You have to be very careful of first impressions when you're looking for a job, Tia, it can make all the difference. You'll need to dress for the job you're applying for. I learned that I didn't need to be so sharp for a position that involved interacting with the community. They looked at my poor ass dressed up and didn't think I could relate."

"Yeah, but you looked good though," I said, raising my hand for a high five.

"I sure as hell did, but I haven't had that suit on since."

"That reminds me, I've got to find a violet dress for Yvonne's wedding this weekend."

"Look deep in your closet, you don't need to waste any money buying something new," Jasmine advised, "Violet can be anything between dark purple and light pink."

"I really don't want to go by myself, I wish I had somebody to share my celebration and spend the weekend with me up in Louisville," I said, feeling alone and unattached, "Everybody will be all coupled up except for me."

"You know Wayne will be there for you if you ask him, and you've got your white boyfriend, Jason, he's always there to do whatever."

"Seriously," I said with sarcasm, "I don't want Wayne embarrassing me and I'm not attracted to Jason in that way."

"What about the guy, Reggie, from Atlanta? I thought you two were still talking."

"We are but I need something I can put my hands on, not somebody who is out of town. I want somebody with me at my party after graduation and I want a date to take to Yvonne's wedding. I'm tired of being lonely and I don't see much out there."

"I hear you, girl, but find a job first. If you think it's hard to find a good man, wait until you start looking for a good job, that's a lot harder to find. I can go out any day of the week turn up my flame and get a man for the evening. But you can do all the right things; look like a gold mine on paper and you still can't get an interview. Take it from somebody who's got a man, concentrate on the job. With or without a man, a woman's got to eat."

"You don't know how I feel because you have a man. I need to be held, and I need some sex as much as I need food."

"You can live without sex, but you won't make it long without some food on the table."

"I don't want to talk about that with you because you don't

know what it's like, you've been with your husband since you were twenty years old. What you can do is give me some suggestions for my after-graduation party."

"I'm sorry, I'll shut my noise, like my grandmother used to say. As for the party, you could have it at the Spoken Word Café or rent a party room at the hotel where your parents plan to stay."

"I don't have that kind of budget, Jazz."

"Jim n' Nicks is really good and it probably fits in your budget. Turn in your paper and we can drive out and get an estimate. We can at least get that settled before you leave for Louisville and when you get to the wedding you can relax and have a good time."

"Now that's what I need in my life, maybe I'll even catch the bouquet."

Chapter Four

I decided to skip the bachelorette party on Friday night and drive up early Saturday for the wedding ceremony. Once they were all drunk they wouldn't even miss me. I thought I could sneak in unnoticed, but no such luck, Yvonne and her crew of bridesmaids busted me as soon as I walked into the hotel lobby at Galt's House. She stomped over to the entrance as soon as she saw me wheel my suitcase towards the attendant.

"Tia, I really thought I could count on you to be down for me and you haven't been there for anything so far," Yvonne fussed, welcoming me after my two hour drive to the hotel venue. "Get checked in and then change as fast as you can, I need you to take care of my guestbook."

"Thanks, Yvonne, for congratulating me on passing my defense, you're not the only one with things going on, I have a life too," I said, getting tired of her selfishness.

"I'm sorry, congratulations, girl, I've been preoccupied with this wedding," she said, "You'll understand when it's your turn to get married."

"How long will that be?" I thought as I rolled my bag onto the elevator after I checked in and went up to my room. I took a long shower and changed into the deep purple gown I had worn as a bridesmaid in a wedding two years ago for another friend that Yvonne didn't know. Thank God it still fit. I picked up the guest book Yvonne had given me in the lobby and went down to be the best hostess I could be.

The wedding was going to be in the courtyard outside. I saw a chair and a table had been placed outside the entrance to the seating area. I sat down and opened the book and laid out a pen just as the guests began to drift in. A photographer walked over and began taking pictures of all the wedding guests as they arrived. He was about six-foot-one, dressed in a beige linen suit, and fine as hell. I enjoyed watching him work but I didn't care for his vantage point.

When there was a lull in the flow I said, "Excuse me, but I don't want to be in every picture with her guests."

"Uh-huh, Yvonne warned me about you, the one with the pretty smile," he said, changing the subject. "If you don't want to be in the photo then I'll have to stand beside you."

It was a line of course but it made me blush.

"I'm Gary," he said, aiming the camera at me, "And you are?"

"I'm Tia," I said, looking straight into the lens.

"Nice to meet you, Tia," he said before he resumed taking pictures of the arriving guests.

Once all of the guests were seated it was time for the ceremony to begin. I watched as the groom and his groomsmen took their places at the front of the altar. Then I heard the chatter of Yvonne and her bridesmaids coming before I saw them gather at the rear gate.

"Help us out," Yvonne whispered to me as I stood at the entrance.

I knew the drill, so I signaled for the pianist to change the music, I counted off fifteen seconds before I told her first bridesmaid to move forward and proceed, and then another fifteen seconds until they were all lined up. I let another thirty seconds pass to build up the anticipation before the flower girl walked up. I nodded for Yvonne and her father to take their places and watched her glide up the aisle in her back-out-to-the-ass wedding gown. Thank the Lord this wasn't being held in a church. I pulled the gate up behind me and took a seat in the rear.

Gary kept making eye contact with me all through the ceremony and smiling like he was my new best friend. I watched him doing his job as he caught all the magic moments on film, the vows, exchanging of the rings, lighting of the candle, the kiss, and then jumping the broom.

"Why was it so hard to get to this place?" I asked under my breath as the recessional began, "What am I doing wrong?"

Gary stood by me as he took pictures of them all coming out and I could smell his cologne as he moved around to get the perfect angle. He stayed near the wedding party as they walked to the ballroom set up for the reception. I followed close behind and when we were inside I headed for a seat adjacent to the bar. That was the ideal place to meet single men.

I sat with my eyes glued to the activities all around me as if I was watching a TV screen. I tried to imagine myself in the starring role and how I would play the scene differently. When my chance came I knew how everything would be right down to the music.

"Thanks for helping me out, Tia," Yvonne said as she made her greetings to her guests around the room, "I know I was a self-centered bridezilla every now and then, but I just wanted this day to be perfect."

"Enjoy you day, girl, if you're happy then I'm happy," I told her as the maid of honor whisked her away to the next table.

"How are you doing, Miss Lady?" one of Yvonne's old uncles asked me, "Why are you sitting over here all by yourself looking so pretty?"

"I'm doing fine, I'm just waiting for somebody," I said, lying.

"Do you want some company?" he asked through his bifocals.

"Not right now, I'll find you on the dance floor later," I said with a promising smile.

I few more elderly, then some heavier than I am came over to flirt. Gary kept his eyes on me and pretended to pout when he saw the others guys approach me or sit down at my table. It made me laugh and somehow I didn't feel so all alone. At the end of the reception he got a drink from the bartender and came and sat down beside me.

"Did you enjoy the wedding?" he asked, handing me one of his business cards.

"If Yvonne wasn't my girl from way back, I wouldn't even be here," I said with a laugh, "I've been to so many weddings lately, probably as many as you."

"So what are your plans after this?" he asked.

"Quite a few of us here went to undergrad together and we're going to hang out tonight, do you want to come?"

"Sure, I'd like to spend some time with you."

"I hear there's a street near here downtown where you can pay $10 and go into five different clubs," I told him.

"That's a plan, let me lock up my equipment and I'll meet you out front," he said.

Ten minutes later we were walking in downtown Louisville.

"So tell me something about yourself," he said, bumping his shoulder into mine as we walked, "Where are you from?"

"I was born and raised in Nashville, but my family lives in a small town around seventy-five miles away. I have just finished my Ph.D. at TSU and I'll be graduating in two weeks."

"That's a huge achievement, congratulations on that."

"Thank you, it took seven years of my life and now I'm ready to live again," I said as we stepped inside one of the clubs.

Gary paid for both of us and we found a table on the other side of the dance floor.

We hadn't been there long when he said, "We came here to dance so let's do it."

"All right then," I said as I stood up and weaved my way through the crowd behind him.

Now I usually don't dance, so to get me out on the dance floor was a miracle. We were out there for a while getting our groove on and then the music changed to a slow jam. We moved closer to each other and when we touched it was like electricity.

He whispered into my ear, "Did you feel that?"

"I don't know what it was but I felt it," I said, savoring the magic, and for the rest of the evening we just kicked it for ourselves on the dance floor.

"Are you ready to leave?" he asked after I unsuccessfully attempted to hide a yawn, the evidence of a long day.

"I am kind of tired," I said regretfully, I never wanted this night to end.

"Come on, I'll walk you back to your hotel," he said, taking my hand and leading me out of the crowded club.

It suddenly dawned on me that we hadn't met up with any of the wedding party and it didn't matter as far as I was concerned. I'm sure they didn't miss me and I definitely didn't miss them. I just soaked in the cool air of my own romantic spring night in Louisville. When I left Nashville this morning I never thought I would be walking down the street all boo'ed up and holding hands with a fine specimen like we'd been a couple for a lifetime. I was floating on air like a bird in flight so it didn't take us long to get back to Galt's House. We stopped at the entrance to exchange numbers.

"I don't want to say goodnight yet," he said.

"I'm enjoying the breeze, let's stay outside and talk for a while," I said, prolonging our time since I was leaving the next day.

It was all so relaxed and easy, we talked and laughed, and we enjoyed some quiet moments where he just held my hand. Before we knew it was 4:00 in the morning.

"I better let you get some rest," he said, standing up and walking me to my room.

"I had a nice time," I said softly.

Then he gave me a deep sensuous goodnight kiss that was like Luther Vandross singing *A House is Not a Home*, "Good morning, good evening, good afternoon, hello, bye bye, baby."

I closed the door behind him and it was all I could do to keep from rushing out and asking him to come back. Hope stayed alive when he called me on the way back to his car.

"Why don't you stay in Louisville tomorrow, hang around for

one more day," he pleaded, but I didn't need much coaxing.

"I don't mind staying but I'm supposed to check out this morning," I said, waiting for his next move.

"Work out the arrangements with the hotel and I'll pay for the extra day," he said, sounding like Blair Underwood in the movie, *Set it Off.*

He showed up after breakfast and took me over to his photography studio and showed me around his set up.

"This is really nice," I said, impressed, "It's good to see a brother handling a business of his own."

"I've got some appointments this afternoon, but I'll be back over to see you after I get done with work," he said as he drove me back to Galt's House.

I was having a great time, this was the break that I needed to help me forget about all the other things I had going on in my life. When he showed up later with food and candles it only got better. He set up a table and lit the candles. I was blown away by the romance of this man, and then we kissed again.

"I was hoping this would happen the first time I saw you," he said, looking me in the eyes while he undressed me.

"I never expected this to happen," I said, feeling the girls tumble out of my bra.

The electricity we felt the night before was just a preview of the explosions that went off in the room that night. I took back all the ugly things I thought and said when Yvonne called me to be a bridesmaid in her wedding. Gary had made the cat yowl, meow, and purr before he was done.

"I've got some early appointments this morning," Gary said after he showered, "Call me before you get on the road."

"I wish I didn't have to go," I told him before he pulled the door closed.

I turned on my mp3 player after I got out of the shower and started singing with Keith Sweat, "who can do you like me, nobody, baby." I sang it all the way back to Nashville.

My faith in love had been restored, I was a believer again. It is possible to find someone who is a total package. I had prayed I wouldn't have to settle and now my prayer had been answered.

"You look happy, Tia," Jasmine said when I sashayed into her office that afternoon, "I expected you to be in a funk when you got back."

"I am feeling Gucci, honey, I do not have a problem with weddings anymore, there is plenty love to go around," I said as I sat down and flashed my prettiest and self-satisfied smile.

"What's up with this? You might as well start talking, because I know it's juicy," Jasmine said, putting her samples back in the freezer and pulling up a chair.

"I met somebody at the wedding and it was all that and a bag of hot chips, and a Pepsi."

"Stop, who, and when did this happen?"

"It was the photographer at Yvonne's wedding," I said, throwing my hands up in the air.

"So you are this gone in two days," she asked, looking at me like I had lost my mind, "I can't believe you went down like that."

"Trust and believe, girlfriend, and I broke all of my rules."

"Tia, now you have me worried," Jasmine said, "This guy lives in Louisville and you live in Nashville, I thought you were done with long distance relationships."

"We can't always control where we meet somebody, I don't care where he lives, and I've got to go because he's calling me right now," I said when I saw his number flashing on my phone.

***

It just didn't get any better, I was graduating tomorrow, the luncheon afterward was scheduled at Jim 'N' Nick's, my mama and daddy were already checked into their hotel, and even though Gary couldn't get here for the celebration because of prior commitments we had been talking on the phone everyday for two weeks. My best white guy friend, Jason, was filling in as my supporter once again at the pre-graduation reception.

Jason had always been there for me since we met in undergrad at TSU. He was the best study partner on campus when we were taking physics and calculus together. He got a job as an engineer at DuPont after we graduated and he was making that good long money. He took me out to eat, moved furniture, and even paid my cell phone bill or car insurance when I was short. He was the perfect man except he was on the heavy side and he didn't make me say ooo wee. I'm not prejudice; he just doesn't turn me on.

"Who's going to hood you tomorrow?" Denise asked while we were seated around the table at the reception in the Barn.

"My dad and Dr. Haynes are doing it. My mom is in a wheelchair and it would be too much drama trying to get her on stage. Plus, I think all the people might freak her out, her nerves are on edge right now."

"The most important thing is that she's here to see you get that paper you've worked so hard for, it has been a journey," Jasmine said, almost making me cry.

"Let's go to B.B. King's tonight," Curtis said when he came by our table.

"I'm down," I said, speaking first, and for once I didn't feel like a charity case.

"I'll see you tomorrow," Jason said politely, leaving the table.

I made sure my mama and daddy were comfortable in their hotel room and then I went to my apartment. I changed into some skinny jeans and a long flowing silver top. It was crowded at the club but we still found a table and when a man who looked like he could be my daddy asked me to dance, I said yes, relieved that the curse of only being approached by older men had finally been broken. I danced my heart out and shook what my mama gave me until Jasmine reminded me I had to be at the Opry House at 9:00 in the morning. I called it a night, drove home, crawled into bed, sent Gary a sexy text, and rolled over and went to sleep.

I could barely tear myself away from the mirror after I put on my regalia in the morning. It was real to me now; I was Dr. Tia King, Tia King, Ph.D. I felt so proud of myself. I had accomplished something that even I had my doubts about from time to time. This was going to be better than any wedding day. I was getting something that no one could ever take from me.

"Tia Annette King" the president called and I did my dignified walk out to center stage. I caught my daddy's eye as they raised the hood over my head and we both teared up.

I teared up again later at the restaurant when my mama kept looking confused when I asked her what she wanted to eat.

"I'll take care of her plate; you go sit down and enjoy your guests," Thomas said, pushing me aside, I guess that was the least he could do.

"We're going to be driving back after this," Daddy said, "Your mama's tired from traveling, don't worry about us, have some fun with your friends."

We made it through the luncheon but the whole vibe had changed when everybody sensed something was wrong with my mama. All I could do was shake my head. The moments of joy in life are so fleeting and the agony never seems to go away. I pasted a smile on my face for the rest of the afternoon.

At home that evening, my phone rang and I finally heard the voice I had been waiting for all day, "Hello, Dr. King."

"Gary, I was just about to call you, I've been missing you," I said, elated.

"How was your day?"

"It had its highs and lows but it was good," I told him, cuddling up on the couch and wishing I was in his arms and he was in my bed.

"I'm sorry, I would have loved to be there."

"Talking to you is making all the difference, I want to close my eyes and pretend you're here."

"I'm feeling the same way," he said, making me feel hot.

"Tell me what you would do if you were here with me," I asked, wanting to hear more.

"I'd start rubbing your feet because I know you've been on them all day. I'd rub your back and neck, and then I'd run you a hot bath."

"That all sounds so good, but I need you to take it to another level."

"I would, but it's too frustrating to talk about it when I can't be with you," he said.

"I'll accept that for now but I need to see you ASAP, let me know when your schedule clears up and we can hook up," I told him.

"I'll do that," he said, "Now get some rest."

I woke up in the same spot the next morning. I felt so drained. I stayed in the house all Sunday to rest and psyche myself up for the job hunt that would begin first thing on Monday.

***

I spent the next two weeks looking on websites at Vanderbilt University, the National Institute of Health, the FBI, and some pharmaceutical companies. I looked for teaching positions at all the local colleges and I even put in an application to student teach for Metro schools. I sent out my CV's to more than twenty-eight positions and I was feeling encouraged. I was knocking on a lot of doors and surely one would open.

After another week, I hadn't gotten any responses and I was feeling anxious hanging around the house all day by myself. Gary was going through his own changes but we were still talking on the phone every now and then, except it seemed like I was doing most of the calling. He was starting to act funny with me and he seemed irritated every time I called. On our last phone call he mentioned that he was having some business problems and for the past few days he wasn't answering any of my texts. I don't know what happened but I decided to let it go for now and give him a chance to work out his issues.

"Have you found a post-doc position," Dr. Gupta asked when she saw me walk down the hall in my old department.

"Not as of yet, but I am about to concentrate my search as we speak," I said.

"I would consider hiring you as a post-doc if you're interested, come by my lab before you leave and I'll give you my grant proposal to read over."

"Thank you for the offer," I said, surprised, "I'll pick it up in a couple of hours."

Dr. Gupta had been one of my professors and she wasn't easy to deal with. I knew I wasn't going by her lab and I should have told her so. I needed to get away from the school. I had been in the department for seven years and I needed to get into a new environment. I had some hard times getting my degree and I was ready to put them behind me. Coming here to the same department everyday working for another nut case would be like Bill Murray in the movie, Ground Hog Day.

Hey look who's here," Jasmine said cheerfully when I walked into the Core, "How's it going on the job search?"

"It's going, I don't know where, but I'm applying for everything."

"That's what you have to do, keep your options open, and something will come through."

"Dr. Gupta just offered me a job on my way in," I said as a joke.

"What did you tell her?" Jasmine asked, all serious.

"I told her I would go by and pick up her grant proposal but I'm not going to."

"Why not, Tia, it's a job. It will keep you on your feet and pay the bills until you find what you really want."

"I don't want to be coming back here every day again like nothing changed. You know Dr. Gupta is crazy and I don't feel like dealing with that insanity, it's not worth it. Besides you know you wouldn't have taken a job working for her either."

"Girlfriend, I have never turned down a job in my life. I have worked doing some things you would not believe. As a black woman you don't have that luxury, especially if you don't have a job right now."

"I am not that desperate, I have time to get the job I really want."

"All right, I'll leave it alone, but it's hard out here. In this economy there aren't a lot of jobs and the competition is fierce," Jasmine said, putting the fear of God in me about finding a position. "When you've got bills, nothing is beneath you."

"Now that you've sufficiently killed any positive feelings I had left I might as well tell you the rest of my disappointment," I said, sighing.

"What are you talking about, Tia?"

"It's Gary, he stopped calling, then he stopped answering, even the texts, and I don't know why," I said, feeling totally dejected.

"I didn't want to say anything before because you were so happy but the whole thing was kind of fishy to me. I didn't understand why he would rather pay for another night at the hotel instead of inviting you over to his place."

"He said it was messy, he wasn't expecting to meet anyone at the wedding."

"All I know is, when a man makes excuses about why you can't come over to his place he's usually married or living with somebody," Jasmine said matter-of-factly.

"That still doesn't explain why he won't answer my calls or texts," I said, frustrated.

"It's over for him, Tia, he wanted some new pussy, he got it, you wanted the dick, and you got it, end of story."

"I wanted more than that and I don't see how he could have treated me so sweet if his heart wasn't in it. Why did he even bother with the phone calls for over a month?"

"Maybe he had an attack on his conscience, but he got over it," she said, "You had some fun and he made your weekend, that's not so bad."

"I think guys must think I'm easy because I'm heavy," I said, feeling more than a little sorry for myself.

"Don't go there, you have never let your weight bother you, so don't start."

"I guess you're right," I said to Jasmine.

Even so, it was hard to let go. In my mind he was my photographer. I only had two days instead of the four days in the movie, "Bridges of Madison Country," but for me they were the best I'd ever had.

5

Chapter Five

"L et it go, we're back out on the prowl again, and I love it," Jasmine said on the phone after listening to me cry the blues some more.

"Not yet, I need a job first," I told her, but really I couldn't believe that I had gotten burned yet again.

I had sworn that I would never get involved with a married man a long time ago. It was at the end of my undergrad years and I was halfway through the process of working at every store of this strip mall on Charlotte Avenue. I started at Burger King, then I moved to Sally's Beauty Supply, and I finished up at Walgreens. I had met this guy named Stephen while I was at Burger King and we became friends. He was the quiet type, light skin, dimples, a deep voice, and was really cute. He would drop by wherever I worked and talk and we stayed in touch even after I graduated. As time went by he would stop by my apartment every now and then and I confess we became friends with benefits.

I was working as a substitute teacher and going through some health problems when he made one of his intermittent phone calls to check on me.

"How you doing today?" he asked casually.

"I'm really sick," I told him, "Both of my legs are stiff and one side of my body is hurting and I can't walk."

"I'll be over there in a few," he said seriously, like he was Fireman Bill and hung up the phone.

He came over to my apartment with groceries and proceeded to cook dinner for me, making me feel like I was the most important person in the world. After that he would do the cooking at his house and bring the food over to me until I got better. He was there for me the whole time I was sick for whatever I needed. I thought he was so sweet and that's when we really started dating and he started staying over at my apartment. There were times off and on when he was out of pocket, but he had a lot of responsibilities. He lived with his mom, stepsister and her kids, and he had to help them out a lot.

For my birthday we met at a restaurant at the Opry Mills Mall. It felt good to be out on the town with him since we spent so much time at my apartment. He made me feel like a queen, ushering me to our table and pulling out my chair. We ordered wine with our meal and while we were eating I noticed his left hand.

"What are you doing wearing a wedding ring?" I asked him with my fork full of food frozen in midair halfway to my mouth.

"It's nothing, there's this girl on my job trying to talk to me and she won't leave me alone," he said, making light of it. "I dug up this ring I had from when I was married to wear to work. I forgot to take it off."

"Is it that serious? Why can't you just tell her that you're not interested?" I asked, confused by the whole thing.

"You wouldn't believe how hard it is to get some women to take no for an answer. They think if you don't want them you must be gay. If you say you're straight then they keep throwing the body at you."

"It sounds suspect to me," I said warily.

"It's nothing; I told you I'm divorced. I wear it to make women leave me alone. Isn't that what you want?"

"Okay, but the next time we see each other I have got to see some divorced papers. If you don't have any, I don't want to see you again until you do," I said in my 'take no shit' voice with much attitude.

A cloud of distrust hung over the rest of my birthday and I wasn't in the mood for the gift of love-making that I had been waiting to receive. I went home and baked myself a cake and sang the birthday song to myself before I drowned myself in calories.

I didn't see him for a few weeks, but when I did I was pleasantly surprised when he laid his divorced papers on the coffee table. Then we were back on again with him making that unfortunate birthday episode up to me with some much needed loving. We became so close that I had a key to his house and he had a key to mine.

Things were really moving forward so I was taken aback and disappointed when he gave me the news, "I'm starting a new job driving a truck, so you might not see me for a while since I'll be on the road."

I soon found out that I couldn't deal with the demands of his new job. I rarely saw him and his phone calls were getting few and farther between. I called him after a week of not hearing from him and all I got was his voice mail. I decided to write him a long letter saying that the new changes weren't working for me and I didn't want to be in this kind of relationship. I dropped it off at his house with the key attached. I was even more puzzled when I still didn't get a response from him. I'm not one to be ignored so after a few more days I called his house again to see if he had gotten my letter.

"Hello," a woman's voice answered courteously.

"Hello, can I speak to Stephen?" I asked.

"He's not here right now," she said.

"Are you his mother or his sister?" I asked, because they often answered the phone and handed it off to him.

"I'm neither one, I'm his wife."

For a few seconds I was speechless.

"Are you going to act like you didn't know?" she asked.

"His wife," I repeated in disbelief, "As far as I know Stephen is divorced."

"Are you playing some kind of game, because I'm not for it?" she said impatiently.

"I'm not playing any games," I said into the phone, "Are you playing games with me?"

"Come on, you are seriously going to act like you don't know."

"I'm not lying to you, I don't know what you are talking about. Stephen told me that he stayed with his mom and sister," I said in my defense.

"Well, I've known about you for a while, but he told me you all weren't seeing each other anymore, and if we were going to make it work I had to trust what he said."

I listened to her in total amazement, grasping that he had made fools out of us. We both got more upset the longer we talked.

"I promise you, I didn't know he had a wife, I made him show me divorce papers."

"I don't know what he showed you but we are married and I am four months pregnant."

"I can show you the letters he gave me if you don't mind me comeing by, I'm not lying."

"Come on by," she said, "I'd like to see them. He assured me that the two of you were nothing more than friends."

In less than fifteen minutes I was knocking at their door but it still didn't make sense. I had been over there to see him on several occasions. When she answered the door with her rounded belly I felt horrible. I handed her the letters and she broke down right there in front of me. She stepped back and sat down on the couch and I walked in and sat down beside her.

"Have you always been here living with him?" I asked, unable to comprehend that he had been that bold.

"Yes, I have, both of our names are on the lease," she answered.

"I called him every morning, and as far as I knew it was his mother or sister who answered the phone and passed it to him."

"No, that was me and I couldn't understand why you called so much except he said you were really sick and didn't have any family."

"What did he tell you when he had my car over here?" I asked curiously.

"He said you were paying him $20 to wash it."

"I have picked him up here and he's gone with me to two of my friend's weddings as my man. I even remember waving to his "sister" in the window."

"I didn't know about any of that, I'm a nurse and I work different shifts."

"He spent so many nights with me at my apartment and I've even spent the night here. When I was here those pictures weren't on the wall. He even brought one of the televisions from here over to my house when mine went out."

She just shrugged her shoulders and I realized that he had taken them off the wall before I got there. Another truth I learned was that she was the one doing the cooking of the food he gave me and he was just bringing me the plates.

Now I understood why his "sister" had an attitude with me and why all the neighbors were mean-mugging me whenever I came over. I just thought he had nosy neighbors.

"I have even picked your kids up from school, your daughter is so sweet," I said dumbfounded, realizing that the little girl was crazy about her daddy's jump-off.

"I was wondering about that when she ran up and hugged you one day," she remarked.

By the time I left, we were both totally blown away. Driving home I wondered what drugs his wife was taking because there was no way I would have passed him the phone with another woman on it every day. That would have never happened in my house, all of us would have had to hang out together. Still, there wasn't much I could say; I had been just as stupid, again.

Stephen had the nerve to call me a few weeks later saying,

"I've been missing you. Can I come by the house and see you?"

"I've talked to your wife," I said, wondering where he got the nerve to call my number.

"You don't need to believe her, she was playing with you."

"You have nothing to say to me," I told him before I hung up.

It looked like history had repeated itself again in my life. I had been suckered in by my need for attention into being played by another married man. I needed to talk to my mama. I needed to know what I was doing wrong, why I keep on making the same mistakes. I wanted to hear her voice tell me that everything would be alright. I wanted to laugh again when she says, "Stop being so desperate."

I picked up the phone and dialed, "Hey, Mama, how are you feeling?"

"Hey, Tia, I've been waiting for you. When will you be coming home?"

"Mama, you know I have been working hard looking for a job, I'm back in Nashville."

"I know. I wish you could find a job close to home, your daddy is working so much and I can't get around like I used too. I need some things from the store."

"Okay, Mama," I said, feeling she was in a different zone today and we couldn't talk.

"I'll see you later," she said, hanging up.

I didn't have her to lean on anymore, she needed to lean on me. I was on my own. I said a quick prayer before I looked in my glove compartment hoping that Wayne had put a few dollars there for gas, but it was empty. I never dreamed that I still would be without a job. My stipend had ended six months ago and the loan I borrowed was almost gone. Here I was worried about having somebody and I couldn't even pay my rent next month.

Instead of heading home, I went by Jason's house. The thought of being at home by myself was too depressing right now.

"Tia, what's up," Jason said when he answered the door, "You usually call me when you're coming by."

"I know but I didn't plan it," I said, "I needed some company and I just took the chance you were home and alone. Is it cool?"

"Yeah, come on in. I got some movies, we can order a pizza, and then you can tell me what's wrong this time."

I hated to admit it but Jason was right, I only came to hang out with him when something was out of order in my life. I needed to do better, friendship isn't a one-way street.

Halfway through the movie and my tummy full of pizza, I said, "My shit has hit the fan, Jason. I can't find a job and I'm almost out of money. My mother is losing it a little more every day, and I think I'm going to have to move back home."

"Do you want to move home?" he asked.

"No, I don't, but I can't pay the rent or my cell phone bill, and I've got to have car insurance."

"You know you can move in with me, Tia," Jason said sincerely, "I can carry your phone and car insurance until you find something."

"I can't let you do that, Jason. You're a good friend and I don't want to spoil it by using you like that."

"It's not using me. I'm your friend, I want to help you out, and I think you would do the same thing for me."

I thought about it for a moment. If I had my shit together and was making good money, I might help him out with a few bills, but he definitely couldn't move in.

"I'll come up with something," I told him, grabbing another slice of pizza.

In the morning I drug myself off of Jason's couch and went home to shower. I called Jasmine to see if she would write me a recommendation for an application I was going to put in at the University of Phoenix. It was one of the few places I hadn't applied.

"What's the good news?" Jasmine asked when she saw my number on her phone.

"I don't have any and I'm feeling discouraged," I said.

"You just need to get away for a minute, take some time off, and get a different perspective."

"I can't afford it right now."

"I'm going to Hot Springs in Arkansas for a couple of days, it's my time to get away by myself. You can ride with me."

"I don't have any money," I responded pitifully.

"I said you can ride with me, you don't need to do anything except help me drive."

***

Getting out on the highway for a road trip reminded me of how long it had been since I had a real vacation. As the miles rolled behind us I left my worries with them, I knew they would be waiting for me as soon as I got back, so I was going to make the most of these days.

"So what is in Hot Springs, Arkansas?" I asked while we

were in route.

"There are the hot springs of course, horse racing, a ferry ride, and a casino," she answered, "That should keep us busy for a few days."

"That's what I need, because when I get back I'm going to have to start making arrangements to move back home."

"Are you sure you can't give it a little more time?"

"No, my money won't let me."

"You might need to reconsider your relationship with Jason, he's a good man, dependable, and he would do anything for you," Jasmine said, crunching on some chips.

"My mother would have a fit, and it wouldn't last, you know I need a Mandingo brother," I said, laughing and hitting the steering wheel.

"You have had your share and look what it has gotten you. It might be time to try something new," she said, looking over her sunglasses. "You're in this rat race because you want to be."

I turned my attention back on the road, this trip was my opportunity to have some fun and clear my head. We checked into the Staybridges Suites, unpacked, and then went out to Red Lobster. I had a gift card that I'd gotten as a graduation gift for the restaurant that I hadn't used yet, so at least I could pay for dinner. The food was good and the atmosphere was relaxing. Afterwards we drove around to take a look at the city.

"Reggie has been texting me, he wants to see me the next time he comes to Nashville," I said offhandedly.

"I like him, but are you sure you want to get involved with somebody who's getting divorced and has kids?" Jasmine asked. "He's got more complications than you do."

"I know, but somehow I can't give up on having somebody of my own."

"You're the one who said they didn't want a long distance relationship," she reminded me, "But I guess texting can't hurt, it'll keep you entertained."

"You don't know the half of it."

"What's that supposed to mean, are you two having phone sex?" she asked, being nosy.

"He sent me some pictures of what he's working with" I said with a giggle.

"Stop," Jasmine said with her mouth hanging open, "What did you think when you saw it, what did you do?"

"I sent him one of me," I said, waiting for her shock to wear off.

"What did you send him?" she asked, looking horrified but enjoying every minute of the conversation.

"The same thing he sent me," I said, watching her eyes roll back in her head.

"The top or the bottom?"

"I sent both," I said, laughing so hard I could barely drive.

"How were you posing?" she asked with her eyes wide open with surprise. "Was it artistic or porno style?"

"Straight up porno style," I said as we pulled into the hotel parking lot, "I showed him all the goodies. That's why he can't wait to get back to Nashville."

"Child, I can't believe you. If you were twenty I would say forget it and wait, but at your age I guess you have to have your fun."

"Now you're feeling me."

"So back to his picture," she said, "Was it all you were hoping for?"

"I'm not saying, and you can't tell that much from a picture anyway."

"This is a new day, honey, and y'all don't have no shame," she said, teasing me, "Sending pictures of your privates all over the airwaves. What if he shows them to somebody?"

"That's why you don't put your face in the picture," I said, "If it shows up anywhere I'll swear it's not me."

"As long as it's not anybody you know, because anybody who knows you and has been there would know it was you."

"Stop trying to scare me, Jazz," I said as we walked into our room, "I'm keeping his secrets so I hope he's keeping mine."

I played some games on my laptop and Jasmine watched movies until midnight. When she went to bed I got on the phone and texted back and forth with Reggie until late in the night. I had only been asleep a few hours when Jasmine was getting up for breakfast.

"You don't have to get up," she said, "But breakfast is free and served until 10:00."

"So what's on the itinerary for today?" I asked after we had eaten and showered.

"This is the day for refreshing and renewing," Jasmine said, "We are going to take the River Boat ride down Lake Hamilton and then we're going downtown to the Bath Row."

It was cool seeing all the mansions that line the lake front as the boat floated by. It was so peaceful seeing the backdrop of the mountains above the water. I looked over at Jasmine soaking in a relaxing moment and I shook my head. I had done all the things that I had been told would bring me the success we all strive for, but now I could see that none of it was guaranteed. I had worked and been in school for damn near twelve years and I couldn't even afford to be riding on this boat.

"That was nice," Jasmine said after the boat docked. "Now for the main attraction, we are going to get in the healing waters of the Hot Springs. We are about to be cured of ailments we don't even know about."

"I have never seen anything like this," Jasmine said when we got downtown.

There were spas and bathhouses lined up and down all the streets. There were so many we didn't know which one to choose. We found a place to park and got out to get a closer look. We chose a bathhouse with statues of white lions on the outside. It looked like it belonged in another country. The attendant told us about the history of the baths and showed us where the hot water bubbles up from the earth and is then cooled down for the baths. We got the $20 package to start with. We didn't need to select the private or romantic settings since it was just us.

"Go over to your left, you can change in there. Shower to remove lotions and deodorants, and then you'll see the door to the baths," the clerk at the desk directed.

I changed into my bathing suit inside one of the changing areas, then I rinsed off in the shower. Inside the bath area there were three pools from 96 degrees to 103 degrees. It was a unique environment. You just find a spot in the bath of your choice and get in. There were people in every pool, but not a lot of talking, it was totally mellow.

"Let's start in the 93 degree area, it sounds hot enough to me," Jasmine suggested.

The water felt so good bubbling up around us, we just sat there and took it all it for a few minutes, then an attendant came by and handed us glasses of the cool spring water to drink.

"This is heaven, I'm hooked," I told Jasmine as we allowed the water therapy to work its magic on us.

"Do you want to take it higher?" Jasmine asked after about a half hour.

"I'm ready when you are," I answered, and then we moved into the 96 degree bath.

Those three degrees made a difference and it took a while to get used to it. I started to sweat so I raised my hand for another glass of cool water. I never would have thought it but it was pleasant to sit and be with perfect strangers while we sat quietly in the mystical waters that were believed to heal and renew. They were black and white, young and old; I imagined all of us were hoping for something particular from what these waters had to offer.

"This is as high as I'm going," I said to Jasmine.

"I hear that, I'm going to give this a few more minutes and then I'm back down to 93 degrees."

"Now I can see what all the fuss is about," I said, "If I lived here I would be a regular. I'd have to split my hair and pedicure budgets to come and sit in this water."

"There's something to it but I can't tell you what it is," Jazz said with her eyes closed.

The rest of the trip went by too quick. It turned out the horses don't race in the summer and that was a disappointment, but we hit the casino and when I won fifty dollars it felt like I had hit the jackpot. I refused to play another quarter.

***

Back in Nashville, the reality of having to move back home to my mama and daddy's house was hitting me like a ton of bricks. Nothing was working out according to plan. I was mad. I got this mutha fucking beautiful ass diploma and none of the shit that's supposed to go with it. Excuse my superlatives, but this is serious. Call 911, Bob Barker, Pat Sajak, Wayne Brady, even old ass Monte Hall, or whoever the hell is in charge because I signed up for the package deal. It includes the diploma, the job, the house and car, the man, and a kid. Notice, I'm not greedy, there is only one child and no dog in the deal.

"Tia, you have enough cooking equipment in here to open up your own Bed Bath and Beyond, you must have a thing for kitchen gadgets," Jasmine said as she and Denise helped me pack up my apartment.

"I do like to bake and I like all the new conveniences. We all have our vices don't we, Miss-New-Pair-of-Shoes every other week."

"There is no need to get testy you two," Denise said, halting our latest sparring match before it got started, "We need to save all of our energy to get this stuff packed up and out of here by tomorrow."

"I can't believe you have so much stuff," Jasmine said, "When I was still in school I practically lived out of a suitcase."

"Excuse me, but how old were you?" I asked her, "I've been on my own for twelve years and living here for damn near eight of them."

"You're right, Tia," Jazz said, patting me on the shoulder,

"I'm going to leave you alone because I can see you are on edge."

"Hell yes, I'm on edge. If I had known I was going to go through all of this and still be struggling to find a job I would have just taken the post office exam."

"Me too, girl," Jasmine laughed, "I would already have close to twenty years in, making more money, and I would have earned a pension too."

"Is it too late?" Denise asked, giving me a dead serious look.

"It is for me, at this point I need to get my money's worth," I told her.

"What are we going to do with your big furniture and all these boxes, they surely will not fit in your car?" Jasmine asked.

"I'm going to have to put most of it in storage here, my parents don't have room for all of my stuff in Pulaski," I said.

"Storage, ouch, that's another bill," Denise added.

"Jason said he'll float it for me for three months," I said, sighing.

"Tia, I'm telling you, we may have to seriously reconsider some things, that man is good to you. You don't find a man like him every day, black, white, yellow, or brown," Jasmine blurted out from behind a stack of boxes.

"I'm going to tell you like I keep telling my mama, it may seem like I'm desperate some times but I assure you that I am not."

"I don't know why people never want the one that wants them," Jasmine remarked out loud.

"That girlfriend is one of the true mysteries of life," I said, taping up the last box.

With all my worldly possessions in storage I headed down Interstate 65 South to Pulaski. Jasmine's words replayed in my mind again. Did I really only have two choices? Do I have to accept the men who are attracted to me or do I wait forever and a day for the man whom I'm attracted to find me? Neither one of those options were very attractive. Is it necessary for me to change who I am to get who I want, or do I just stay by myself?

Chapter Six

As the miles clicked up on the odometer I got more depressed. I wasn't ready for all the questions. Pulaski is a small town and everybody was going to want to know why I came back. I'm supposed to be all that. Why would I have to come home to live with my mama and daddy? I wasn't about to tell people that I couldn't find a job. Surely, I'm not the only person who can ride back into town with a Ph.D. and feel like an absolute failure? I parked in front of the house and sat there a few minutes before I went in.

"Hey, Mama, I'm here," I called out, after I finally got the nerve to go in the side door.

"Tia, I'm so glad you're back home," Mama called back to me from the living room, "Your daddy already left for work."

I walked in the living room to see her and it hurt my heart. I froze in my tracks without even giving her a hug. Mama's legs were so swollen and the skin looked dark and stretched as if it would tear at any moment. Maybe it was a good thing that I had to come back home, nobody was taking care of Mama like she needed, she shouldn't be left alone.

"We need to get you back walking around again as soon as

we can, Mama. You know I probably won't be here that long. Have you been watching your salt intake, your legs look like you're retaining water? Are you still on water pills?"

"Stop with all the questions. I'm better now since I won't have to worry about you up there in Nashville with all them crazies."

"When's the last time you went to the doctor?" I asked, still concerned about her legs.

"I don't know, chile, the doctors don't do anything for me. They get on my nerves."

"I'm going to make an appointment for you," I told her, looking up the number on my laptop. Daddy probably hadn't taken her since the last time I was home. When he wasn't at work he was usually asleep. I knew she could be hard to get along with and her being sick sure didn't make it easier. He took care of all the bills, but he pretty much went his own way. I've never asked what went down between them but Mama hadn't forgiven him and now he didn't care anymore. Thank God, Daddy was old school enough not to walk off and leave her for somebody else.

***

Dr. Burton's nurse wheeled Mama into the examination room and I waited outside thumbing through a magazine until he was done.

After 30 minutes or so he stepped outside the door and said, "Come into my office with me, Ms. King, so we can talk for a few minutes."

I followed him down the short hallway to his office. I sensed that the news wasn't good because he was talking with me in his office away from where my mother could hear.

"Ms. King, your mother's condition is not going to get any better and as time passes she will need more care and eventually she will require the twenty-four care of a nursing home. We need to begin to prepare her for the transition. She's very emotional so it's going to be a task to convince her that this will be the best decision for her care."

"What are we talking about, Dr. Burton, is the condition of her legs permanent?" I asked fearfully.

"Your mother has several things going on with her, there are the complications from her diabetes and she's experiencing some dementia. Neither of these diagnoses can be reversed and will deteriorate further as time goes on."

"I don't know anything that can be said that will convince her to go into a nursing home. I'll probably be the one who has to care for her?"

"I'm sure you have a job or a career that will make it impossible for you to be with her all day every day," he said matter-of-factly.

I held my tongue, I couldn't bring myself to tell him I didn't have a job or a career at the moment.

"Thank you, Dr. Burton, I think we'll take things one day at a time, we don't have to make a decision right now. If the situation changes drastically then we'll make the necessary adjustments."

It didn't take long for me and Mama to develop our routine, breakfast in the morning, then the dishes, check my e-mails, Facebook, and then Linked-in. I would make us some lunch around 1:00 and we watched a lot of Court TV. In the afternoon, I did the shopping if we needed anything or called my girls to stay caught up on the gossip. Then I cooked dinner and we watched some more TV game shows. The next morning I got up and repeated the whole thing. I broke the monotony with sexual banter with Reggie on my cell phone, better known as sexting, and it was getting me worked up.

"Your pictures look so sexy," he told me, "I think about you all the time."

"Tell me what you think about," I asked, wanting to hear more details.

"I think about kissing you and caressing your body, feeling your warmth and making love to you all night."

I would send him another picture whenever I needed to hear more of the compliments. Not having a job was messing with me. I felt insecure and rejected. Listening to Reggie made me feel attractive and wanted. Aside from the fact that it had been a while since I had knocked any boots and I was jonesing. The thought of lying next to this incredible black hunk of man was starting to keep me up at night. So when Reggie mentioned that he would be in Nashville and he wanted to see me, it was music to my ears. Sweet music like the first time I heard him sing. I had seen and heard a lot over my cell phone and I was ready to take it to the next level.

"I don't have any income right now," I told him, not wanting to appear too eager but knowing I was going to make it work somehow.

"I got you, Tia. I'll pay for your gas and everything else. Pack you weekend bag and get in the car, I want to spend some time with you."

"You know I'm taking care of my mom right now," I said hesitantly.

"Can't you make some arrangements for a couple of days? I know you could use a break."

"What time will you get done making your round of sales calls?" I asked.

"I should be done around 3:00, or call me when you get in town and I'll stop on a dime."

"I'll work something out with my dad on taking care of Mama. I can fix everything where she can make it until he gets home and then he'll be off from work the next day. I should be able to get there around 5:00 tomorrow.

"I can't wait to see you, Tia." he said, making me smile from ear to ear.

I called Jasmine at work. "You're going to die when I tell you this," I said, knowing she likes to hear all about my juicy love connections.

"You got a job, where is it," she said, getting excited.

"No, it's not a job, its Reggie. He wants me to meet him in Nashville tomorrow and stay with him for a couple of days."

"Are you going to come, what about you mother?" she asked.

"I'm coming. My daddy is going to be here with her so I can get a break."

"Now that's what I'm talking about, you got to get a piece every now and then. A woman your age doesn't need to do without."

"I want to tell you to get your mind out of the gutter, but you are right, girl, it has been too long," I said, laughing.

***

In the morning over breakfast I told Mama, "I'm going to Nashville for a couple of days. After lunch I'll clean up and get you settled and Daddy will be home in a few hours."

"What are you going to Nashville for? Do you have a job interview?" she asked

"No, Mama, I going to see some friends and clear my head for a couple of days," I said, looking down at my food. My real plans made me feel guilty.

"Well, have a good time and make sure you call me when you get there," she said.

I was relieved and disturbed at the same time that she didn't tease me about going to see some man, being desperate, or ask where I was going to stay.

I got a text from Reggie saying he was staying in a hotel near West End with the address and room number typed at the bottom. I know Nashville like the back of my hand but I still loaded the address in the GPS. When it announced that I had reached my destination I was confused. The hotel where he was staying off of West End Ave turned out to be a Days Inn motel on Charlotte Ave. It had taken a lot of maneuvering and driving to get here so I refused to let it dampen my mood. He opened the door after the second knock and I walked into his arms. I almost laughed out loud when the words 'I just want to be held' floated through my mind.

"Long time no see," I said, putting my bag down.

"Too long, but we're finally here now, that's all that matters," he said, rubbing my back and closing the door behind me.

"So what do you have planned?" I asked, hoping he wouldn't give me the typical male response of "What do you want to do?"

"We can do whatever you want," he answered.

I guess it was too much to hope for so I said, "I'm hungry; let's go get something to eat."

We drove around for a while in rush hour traffic looking around and then he pulled up into a McDonald's parking lot.

"Is this a joke?" I asked myself silently.

Now believe me, I have eaten my share of Mickey D's and I don't have a problem with it, usually, but it definitely wasn't what I had in mind after driving seventy-five miles to see this Negro.

"Do you need to use the restroom or is this where we're eating?" I asked him with as little indignation as I could.

"You don't like it?" he asked, having the nerve to act surprised.

"It's not that I don't like it, it's just not what I expected," I said, giving him a questioning look in the eye that asked, "Are you for real?"

"I want to take you someplace nicer. I really want to roll out the red carpet for you, but my money is funny this weekend and I just had to see you. My ex is taking me through changes about getting the kids ready to go back to school in a few weeks, so I gave her most of what I planned to spend on you so they could have what they needed."

"I'll let you slide this time, only for the kid's sake," I said, trying not to laugh at the ridiculousness of the whole situation. "But you're going to have to get the food to go; I am not sitting up in there eating with you like we're in a restaurant."

"No problem," he said, pulling up to the drive-thru window and pulling out his wallet.

"Why you're in the wallet, why don't you give me the gas money you promised me before you get me stranded here," I said, half-joking but with my open palm extended.

He pulled off two twenty dollar bills and laid them in my hand. It was barely enough to cover the gas and no change left for a cold drink. I looked at them, folded them up, put them in my handbag, and held my tongue. He had to smile and I felt good about myself for not humiliating this brother. He was a grown-ass man with a job who invited me to drive in town to get busy with him and he had the nerve to take me to McDonalds and I'm damn near 35 years old. I looked around for a newscam because this shit needed to be reported.

There was no use suggesting anything else, we had already hit rock bottom. The only option left was to go to the park and pretend we were on a picnic or got back to the motel. I decided to try to stick to the script I had imagined and prayed that eating in the park would bring the romance back into this scene.

"Let's go by the park, find us some shade, and eat. We can feed the ducks if we have anything left," I said, trying to salvage the bad beginning.

"Thank you," he said to me as we grabbed our combo meals and walked over to a picnic table in the shade under a magnolia tree."

"For what?" I asked.

"For coming and being understanding," he answered.

"I can't blame you for having short finances; mine are all out of order right now," I said, laughing, "Let's hope things get better for both of us real soon."

Once I got over the initial shock I relaxed. Centennial Park was in full bloom and I was happy to be one of the many couples there instead of the single ones for a change. I glanced across the table during the conversation while we ate and he looked delicious. My dried up quarter pounder with cheese and cold fries didn't matter because he was what I was hungry for. The anticipation was building and I felt my mouth watering so I took a swig of Coke to wash it down and cool myself off.

We took a relaxing walk to look at the ducks in the pond even though we didn't have anything left to feed them. Reggie was a real brickhouse, well over six-feet-tall with a thick build. Beside him, at five-feet-two, I was petite, a damsel in distress, and he was my knight in shining amour.

"I don't want to waste any more of my time alone with you," he said, leading me back to the car. "I'm ready to go back to the room."

I just smiled; I didn't want him to know that I was thinking the exact same thing. I kept my gaze out of the side window because I didn't want him to see I was smiling all the way back to the motel. As soon as he closed the door behind us he grabbed my breasts from behind.

"I've been waiting for you to release the girls," he said in my ear with his breath blowing down my neck, "I haven't sucked on any this big before."

It shocked me a little but his passion for me was a turn on. The room wasn't a suite so it wasn't far for us to get to the bed. We kissed and kissed, taking off pieces of clothing between them. I couldn't wait to get my hands on the surprise package so I unfastened his pants and he slipped them off. I pulled down his boxers and something was wrong.

I had seen the preview of what he was working with and I
know I saw more than this. Had it been trick photography?
I prayed silently that it wasn't all the way hard yet and my
fantasy would not be destroyed. It was the same persistence
that got me through graduate school that wouldn't let me
accept defeat. I rubbed and I caressed, I pulled and I tugged,
and to put it politely I used everything I had, but he still came
up short.

"You okay?" he asked when I gave up the fight.

"Yeah, I just need a minute, I'm a little nervous."

"I can get you relaxed," he said, massaging me all over.

I went through the motions and he seemed to be pleased but I
was let down. I was looking forward to something great and it
was only all right. It wasn't that he was a bad lover, he wanted
to satisfy me, but he just didn't have the equipment. I know it's
not always about size and I'll admit that I'm not perfect and
I shouldn't be this hypercritical. So sue me; I expected more
from a man of 6'4". That was nothing but Mother Nature
committing false advertising.

"I'm going to take a shower," I said, climbing out of the bed.

"I'll join you," he said, coming behind me and patting me on
the butt.

I could have used a few minutes alone to get my mind right
but I wasn't going to get them. I stood in front of the mirror
over the sink and searched in my bag for my shower cap. I
could feel his eyes watching me and I was so ready to grab
my phone and dial 911 because I felt like I'd been robbed
or deceived. It was a clean-cut case of breach of trust at the
minimum. I felt hot tears mix with the flow of water on my face

in the shower because I must be truly lonely and desperate to let that slide. Being under-endowed used to be a deal breaker for me, hands down, and I was still here.

"Why don't you turn on the TV?" I asked while I lotioned my skin.

"Why do you want to watch TV?" he asked, smiling with his body spread out on the bed like he was John Shaft, "Am I not entertaining enough for you?"

"I'm self-conscious with it being so quiet in here, somebody might be able to hear us through the walls," I said, needing a distraction.

"It doesn't bother me, I want them to hear what I got going on in here," he said, raising the volume of his voice up to make a public announcement.

I gave him my most serious dead-pan look and he reached for the remote and pushed the power button. I needed the noise from the TV to help me quiet my thoughts. I was worried about how my Mom was doing; I know my Dad is not the most attentive person in the world. I wanted to check my e-mails and find a response to one of my applications. The most important thing was the mental note I made, never have sex with someone for the first time when you are out of town and staying in their motel room, there's no easy out if there's a problem.

"You smell so good," he said, burying his head deep in my breasts.

"It's the same scent you're wearing," I said with a laugh, "It's called soap."

He kissed me and it was lovely, and I was thankful for that, but I could feel his little friend getting excited. I started to think again, Reggie was four years younger than me, and I trembled with the fear that this Negro could go all night.

"Was that an aftershock, baby?" he asked with the confidence that he had truly laid it down.

"Oh yeah," I answered, playing along, "How did you know?"

"A man can always tell when he hits that spot."

I let it go, what good would it do to tell him that he hadn't reached it. My plan was to have a huge orgasm that was so strong that it knocked me unconscious for the rest of the night; unfortunately that's not how it worked out. Nonetheless, we finally fell asleep.

I woke up in the morning starving, all that bumping and humping had done for me was work up my appetite. I got up, showered, and dressed in the bathroom.

"What are you doing dressed so early?" Reggie asked.

"I'm hungry; I'm going out to get something to eat."

"I'm taking care of you while you're here, Tia," he said, getting up, "You sit down and chill, I'll go out and get you some breakfast."

He went in the bathroom for a minute, threw on some clothes, dashed across the room, grabbed the door knob and was halfway out the door before I could say anything.

"I can ride with you," I said, wanting to get out of the room so I could breathe some fresh air for a while.

"No, that's all right, I'll be back in a few," he said, closing the door behind him.

"Damn," I said to myself as I stood at the window, "He didn't even ask me what I wanted to eat."

I took the time he was gone to call home and talk to Mama.

"Hey, Mama, how are you doing this morning?" I asked, relieved when she answered the phone.

"I'm good, Tia," she said, sounding upbeat, "Are you at work already?"

"No, I'm visiting a friend in Nashville. Have you had your breakfast yet?"

"Your Daddy is making my plate right now. I want to eat it while it's hot so I'll call you back or I'll see you when you get home, bye bye," she said, rushing me off the line.

As hard as I was trying to get employed, I was hesitant about leaving my mama, the truth is I'm scared that when I come back to visit her she won't know me. I couldn't bear thinking about it. I was sitting there staring at the cell phone in my hand when the door swung open.

"That didn't take too long did it?" Reggie asked cheerfully with his hands filled with Krystal bags, "I didn't know if you wanted eggs over easy or scrambled, sausage or bacon, toast or biscuits, so I got some of all of them."

"I'll eat all of them, so what are you having?" I asked him, grabbing the bags.

"I'm not worried; you can't eat all of that."

"I could but I'm trying to lose some weight," I said, placing a small amount of each on the plastic lid.

"You don't need to change a thing," he said, scooping up the remainder of the breakfast.

"You do need to score some brownie points today," I told him, appreciating the compliment. "So what are your plans today?"

"I've got some calls to make this morning at Vanderbilt and then I'm all yours," he said.

I started to make a suggestion about where we could meet when his cell phone rang. He looked down on the screen and then he stepped out of the room to talk. A red flag went up. Who is he talking to, and why did he have to leave the room for the conversation? In my mind only a woman on the line would require this much privacy.

"I think that was disrespectful," I said, peeved, when he came back in the room.

"What are you talking about?" he asked, playing dumb.

"You took a call from another female while you were with me and then you walked outside so you could talk freely or in other words pretend you are not here with me."

"It was my ex, remember we have two kids together, I have to talk to her sometimes."

"Are they conversations that need to be private?" I asked suspiciously. "I feel like you're trying to play me and I don't need that right now. I'm not about that life. Besides, I'm not in the mood for any of this anymore. When you leave out I'm going home."

"Come on, Tia, don't be like that, we waited a long time to hook up," he said, moving over to sit by me on the bed.

"It's bad timing, your money is funny and I'll feel like you're playing me cheap."

"I'm sorry about that but you said you understood my situation."

"I do to a certain extent, and I've been understanding about one thing after another since I got here and now my patience is a little short."

"Well I've got to go, but I hope you'll be here when I get back," he said, giving me a kiss on the cheek.

There was no way I was going to be there when he got back, he had it all twisted. I wish I could say that I had never been so disappointed but that would not be true. I had set myself up again in a situation where the truth wasn't quite clear. I started to call my mama again, but I dialed Jasmine's number instead.

"I'm on my way back home," I said, feeling like I had wasted my time.

"What's the matter, I thought you were going to stay two days?" she asked with a bit of worry in her voice.

"Things didn't really work out the way I hoped they would so I'm going back early."

"Is your mom okay?" she asked.

"Yeah, she's the same, I'm just a little disappointed, and kind of mad too," I said, going through the second phase of my grieving process over my rendezvous.

"What happened, Tia? Stop being so mysterious, spill you guts, girl. Did Reggie show up?"

"Yeah, I guess you could say that most of him did?"

"In one more minute I'm going to jump through this phone and proceed to strangle you," Jasmine said, losing patience with my guessing game.

"Okay, first, I don't know if he's broke or just cheap, but either way I can't deal with a man who has less money than I do. This mofo asked me to drive seventy-five miles and meet him in town for a chance to get in these panties and he had the nerve to feed me Mickey D's."

"You have got to be kidding me; he could have put $10 with it and taken you to O'Charley's or Logan's. He should be embarrassed."

"I'm the one that's embarrassed because I should have turned around and gone back home seeing as it didn't get any better from there."

"Don't tell me he didn't put it down like he was supposed to?" she asked with exasperation rising in her voice.

"All I'm going to say is that it wasn't great."

"What do you mean it wasn't great, what was wrong? If he came with the proper equipment you can make the rest happen," she said, not having a clue.

"It wasn't what I thought it would be," I said, being cryptic.

"Are you talking about the size or the length or something else? I thought he sent you pictures."

"Let's just say they were deceiving."

"It's not always about the size; he could still be a good lover. What was the problem?"

"Jazz, stop being so damn nosy," I blurted out angrily. "I'm not going to give you a blow by blow description of what happened. If you were supposed to know all about it then you would have been there."

"Excuse me, child, with all that attitude he definitely didn't handle his business. Are you sure you shouldn't hang around and give him a chance to get it right?" she asked, laughing.

"Hell no, he pissed me off this morning," I said, getting irritated all over again.

"What got you mad this morning, did he wake up soft and small?" she asked, cracking herself up again.

"Whenever you get done trying to be funny, I'll continue," I said to get her to sober up.

"I'm sorry, girlfriend, this is so good and we are going to

laugh about this in a week or two. Now tell me what he did to make you mad this morning?"

"His cell phone rang after he brought me breakfast from Krystal's and I believe it was another female because he went outside to talk."

"It could have been his ex calling about something, maybe you overreacted."

"That's what he said, but I don't know who it was or what they wanted. All I know is that I felt like a two-dollar ho' sitting up there in a cheap motel room while he stood outside talking to another woman. I can't deal with that shit, I'm done.

"I'm telling you that for a woman to be with any man there are going to be compromises, that's just life."

"I have told you many times, I'm not ready to settle yet, and I don't feel I should have to."

"I hear you, but I know one thing, if 'sad sack' had knocked it out last night you would be singing another tune this morning and you would wait for his ass all day in that bed-bug and flea-infested room for a chance to be knocked out again in round two."

"You're crazy, girl, but you got that right," I said, and I couldn't help but laugh.

"Call me later when you get home because I know he is going to give you an ear full when he comes back to his empty motel room," Jasmine said before she hung up.

I felt better when I got on the interstate headed home with the wind from the open window blowing through my hair. It had been an interesting twenty-four hours and at least I did get a chance to release some tension.

7

Chapter Seven

"Tia, I thought you had to work today," my mama said as soon as I walked in the door. Her short term memory seemed to be getting worse every day.

"No, Mama, I went to Nashville to see some friends and find out what's going on, I'm still looking for a job."

"Did you have a good time?" she asked.

"It wasn't all bad," I answered, thinking back to a particular moment.

"Your daddy said you got some mail, it's on the kitchen table."

Curious, I hurried into the kitchen to see what had come. Hallelujah! God is good; one of the letters waiting for me was from Dr. Hartmann at North Carolina University in Raleigh-Durham. I was more than thrilled; it was the first bite I had gotten from all the CVs and resumes that I had sent out. They wanted me to call them and schedule a time for a phone interview.

"It's about time," I yelled at the top of my lungs. If I handled it properly it would be the prelude to a visit to the campus to interview for a post-doctoral position.

I was in the middle of my celebration when my phone rang. I

looked at the number and it was Reggie. I pushed the button to answer, I couldn't wait to talk to him. He had treated me like a loser and I was a winner, damn it.

"Hello," I said in my sweet voice, "How did your sales calls go, did you make some money?"

"They went well, however, it was a letdown when I got back to the room and you weren't there. I was hoping you would have stayed. I know you were upset and I wanted to make it up to you."

"You don't have anything to make up to me," I replied, "I think the timing was off, but I was offended when you left the room to talk to another woman. In my opinion if you can't speak freely in front of me then you don't take the call."

"I'm sorry about that, I learned something today."

"I was thinking while I drove back that we should pump the brakes on this and back up a little. I really need to focus my energy on getting my career going and see where I'm going with that. Getting into a relationship right now would be too distracting, and I've got my mother to worry about. My plate is full and I'm sure you have a lot going on trying to get things settled with your ex, your children, and getting your finances together."

"I don't believe you're going there with me, Tia. I know I messed up, but it wasn't that serious. We can get past it. I want to help you find a job and deal with whatever else you have on you. I wanna be you man."

"I appreciate that and we can still talk, but let's hold up on the rest. When we both get our situations worked out then maybe we can hook up under better circumstances."

"All right, we'll talk then," he said, annoyed. Then he hung up.

"That's a relief, I've wrapped that up and we're still cool," I said, satisfied with myself. "I'm just not feeling him. I not a gold-digger but I'm not messing with no broke nigga."

The next thing I needed to do was google the University of North Carolina and their research programs. Then I needed to research Dr. Hartman, find out what he's written and what accolades he has received. After that I needed to go to Pubmed and pull the publications that have come out of his lab in the last three years. I wanted to be prepared. I've been caught off guard lately and I don't play that.

It's the morning of my phone interview and I am excited. I scheduled it for 11:00 so I would have Mama's breakfast taken care of already. She would be already watching Judge Mathis, the dishes would be done, and I would have time to shower and change. I want to be ready, dressed like I was sitting there in the room with them. I want to come through this phone in full effect, top notch, with my winning attitude ready.

"Mama is that the channel you want on the television?" I asked her before I went in the kitchen to make the call.

"Yeah, baby, that's the one, first Judge Mathis and then Judge Joe Brown."

"Do you need anything, snacks or water, and are you cool? Because for about 30 minutes I'm not going to be disturbed and I can't answer you if you call me."

"I'm fine, Tia, go on and do what you got to do," she said, turning to the TV screen.

"Well, I'm going to my interview then," I said, walking back to my room.

I look in my dresser mirror and I'm feeling fly, my hair looks good but my lipstick needs to be retouched. I start to feel nervous and jittery as I press the numbers on my phone because this means so much to me. It is so disheartening when friends and fellow students ask me if I've found a job yet. I'm tired of answering, no, I'm still looking or I'm waiting on a response. I know it's a bad economy and competition for jobs is fierce but this is not what I expected. The number starts to ring and I feel that this could be my blessing.

"Be with me, Lord, through this phone call," I prayed out loud as the number rang.

"Hello, this is Tia King; I have a telephone interview scheduled with Dr. Hartman."

"Yes, he's expecting your call, I'll transfer you," a female voice I assumed was his administrative assistant said.

"Good morning, Ms. King, I'd like to keep this a relaxed and casual conversation so I'd like you to call me Steve, and I hope you won't mind if I call you Tia.

"No, that's fine with me," I replied, glad he wasn't one of those pretentious investigators who need to be called doctor all day.

"Also, there will be two other people from our department that will be sitting in on the call, Jill Banks and Patrick Lu; they may have some questions for you or they can answer any questions you may have while we're talking."

"That sounds great," I said, happy that it would be one call versus three separate calls. "I'm glad to speak with you all this morning. I'm very excited to discuss the opportunity."

"So, Tia, why don't you tell us about your interests and what you visualize as your long-term goal," Dr. Hartman said.

"As you probably have read in my CV, my research interests and experience have been centered on the c-myc gene and tumor suppression. I have read your articles and I can see where I can connect my research and take it to the next step. Long-term, I have a number of interests, I can see myself going into forensic science, but I'm open to several directions that this experience may take me. Basically I'm a hard worker and I want to keep my options open."

"There are a number of paths where I can see your research branching out, which was one of the reasons that you were chosen from the large group of submissions," Steve replied.

"What is your preference as far as the work environment is concerned?" a female voice I assumed was Jill's asked.

"I enjoy meeting new people, the size of a lab doesn't matter to me, and I don't have a problem working independently. I communicate well with those around me and I'm ready to get out there and get busy and productive again.

"Hi, Tia, this is Patrick. I was wondering if you have ever visited this part of the east coast? We're a very diverse group here. Do you have any qualms about working with different people from various backgrounds?"

"I've been in diverse environments my whole life. I worked my way through school in customer service jobs and I have a knack for working with people. I think that diversity leads to a more successful atmosphere where people are able to come from an assortment of areas with different ways of thinking. It provides a mix that has something extra with the varying points of view that come together. Diversity is not an issue for me at all."

The interview goes on from more technical questions to the weather and things to do when you're not working.

"Well, Tia, do you have any more questions or comments for us?" Steve asked.

"You all have been very thorough in answering all my questions. For me, I have been down a long road to get to this point and I'm anxious to get some new things accomplished."

"That's sounds very good," Steve said. "It has been great speaking with you and having the opportunity to get to know you better and hear where your interests lie. We have three post-doctoral positions that we need to fill and we have five candidates that we will be choosing from. What we'd like to do, as we all sit here and nod in agreement, is have you to come over for a weekend, show you around, have you do a presentation for us, if that sounds good to you."

"That sounds excellent to me, I love that idea. I'm all for it," I said, pleased that they wanted me to come.

"All right then," Steve said, "We'll get all the details worked out here and have our administrator get back with you and coordinate the arrangements. We look forward to seeing you within the next few weeks."

"I thank you so much for this opportunity and I will see you all very soon," I said in my calm and professional voice before I hung up. "Oh, my goodness, hallelujah," I yelled out once I was sure the line was disconnected. "I nailed it, I nailed it!"

Now I was finally getting somewhere, something had moved forward. I didn't know how much longer I could have waited for my first interview. I had gotten through it and I was on my way to North Carolina for a second interview. I headed out to tell Mama the good news.

"You like nice, Tia, where are you going?" she asked when I walked into the living room where she was watching another one of her judges.

"I'm not going anywhere, Mama. I just got myself together physically so I could be together mentally for my phone interview and it went fantastic. I just got finished and they want me to fly there for a live and in color interview."

"Good for you, baby, when are you going?" she asked with her eyes focused back on the TV screen.

"It will probably be within the next few weeks," I said, even though I could tell that I no longer had her attention. I was going to have to repeat it several more times anyway so I let it go. "Do you need anything right now?" I asked her, standing in front of the TV, "I'm going to make a few more phone calls."

"Yeah, baby, can you get me something cool to drink?" she answered, anxious for me to move from blocking the screen."

I walked into the kitchen and poured her a glass of sweet tea, it wasn't good for her sugar but that's what she wanted. I didn't know how to deny her the things she wanted that weren't good for her. I could see she had lost so much already, her mobility, her independence, and now her memory was fading. I handed her the tall glass and went to my room and closed the door. Life just isn't fair I thought for the umpteenth time.

"Guess who rocked their phone interview this morning," I sung to Jasmine as soon as she answered her phone, "I am so geeked right now."

"Well give me the entire story so I can join your celebration," she said, getting hyped.

"The call lasted about a half hour. There were two other people there for a conference call and I was cool, professional, and congenial. When we got done, Dr. Hartman invited me to come over to UNC to have another interview."

"It's about frigging time," Jasmine screamed. "They say trouble don't last always, but sometimes it lingers a little too long and makes you wonder. That is so encouraging. Now I think I'll send out another ton of my resumes."

"I really think I have a good chance, there are five candidates competing for three jobs."

"I like those odds, girl. I think you're going to be a winner, get Curtis Mayfield up on YouTube, it's time to sing your theme song," she said, making me laugh.

"They want me to do a presentation though," I said soberly, remembering how nervous I get speaking in front of a group.

"That's no problem," she said, "Cut your defense down to thirty minutes and roll with it. You don't need to stress yourself out preparing anything new and you don't want to talk too long and lose your audience."

"You're right, I need to focus on what I'm going to wear," I said.

"Choose comfort over style, you don't want anything tight or binding that will make you feel self-conscious about all the eyes on your big booty."

"Bye, Jazz, that's my cue to hang up," I told her before I pushed the end button on my phone.

Now I'm wishing I had stayed on my Weight Watcher's

program. I've probably gained back the few pound I lost before I moved back home. I know I have been stressed out since I've been here, and when I'm stressed I eat, it's a nervous thing. Hopefully I can still fit into my black slacks and one of my dresses and I'm good to go. I'd hate for the way I'm dressed to ruin the good impression I've made so far.

***

It was three days later before the administrator from the Molecular Biology Department at UNC called.

"Is this Tia King?" she asked after I said hello.

"Yes it is," I said, trying to contain my excitement.

"This is Kathryn Houston from the Molecular Biology Department at UNC, I'm calling to confirm your travel arrangements."

"Yes, I've been expecting your call."

"First, I want to make sure that you are still interested in the post-doc position."

"Absolutely, this is an ideal opportunity for me."

"I also need to make sure that you have not accepted another offer."

"No I haven't," I said, surprised at all the questions.

"Well there are a few things about the position that I need to inform you about. The fellowship is offered on a one-year contract that is renewable for a second year and the possibility of acquiring a training grant. The salary is $41 thousand per year. If that is acceptable to you I'll give you your itinerary."

"That's all acceptable to me," I answered, even though all I could think of was that the salary was ridiculous. My daddy made more than that working in a factory.

Kathryn's voice seemed to fade and the volume diminished along with my enthusiasm as I thought about how hard I had worked and what I thought I deserved. Words coming through the receiver giving me times and places interrupted my reverie and brought me back.

"I'm going to send you all the details in an e-mail," Kathryn said, "If there are any problems or conflicts don't hesitate to call me and we'll get them worked out."

"I don't anticipate any problems. Thank you so much and I look forward to visiting the campus," I said, trying to sound upbeat.

I couldn't put my phone down. Kathryn Houston had barely hung up before I was calling Denise. The common objective among all of us was getting that first job after graduation. Now that I thought about it we didn't discuss salaries very much. At this minute that was the only thing I wanted to talk about.

"Hey, Denise, I got the call to go out to UNC but the salary is only going to be $41 thousand," I said, without containing my discontent. "That sounds a little low to me. I don't mean to be nosy but I have to know how much they're paying you at TSU."

"I started off at $40 thousand, Tia, so that is probably a fair offer for your first post-doc position," she said matter-of-factly.

"That doesn't make much sense to me," I said, disappointed to hear that I didn't have an indignant leg to stand on. "I'm going to make a few calls to some people I know in industry. Thanks for the info, girl."

Next I checked with a fellow graduate, Monique, who was working at Vanderbilt and it was the same story. Then I called my girl, Carmen, who was working in a forensics lab in Texas, and her starting salary wasn't encouraging either. I was pretty resigned to the fact that once again I wasn't going to get a piece of the pie in the sky but I called my boy, Jeffery, who worked in DC at the National Institute of Health just to make sure.

"What's up, Jeff," I said when he answered.

"Tia, how you been, lady? I thought you lost my number," he said, sounding surprised.

"No, I've been busy trying to make some things happen and my mother has been sick," I said, making excuses.

Jeffery graduated two years before me. He was cool and tried to talk to me a few times but he wasn't my type. He was always nice, a big teddy bear, and a good brother. The problem was I like a husky man but Jeff was point-blank fat, and that doesn't turn me on. I'm sure most people think I got a lot of nerve taking that position at my size, but I know what I like.

"Are you calling me to say that you regret not hooking up with me and you want to come up for a visit to make it up to me?" he asked jokingly.

"No, you are so silly, Jeff," I said, laughing at his humor, "I wanted to talk to you about the pay rate for post-docs."

"That's a relief, because a lucky lady up here has snatched me up and I'm going down the aisle to put a ring on it in a Christmas wedding," he said, sounding happy, "I couldn't wait on you to come to your senses forever."

"I knew I should have stopped at the last phone call," I thought before I said, "Congratulations, I'm happy for you. I told you that you would find the right one to truly appreciate you."

"You were right, it's all good. So what did you want to know about pay rates?" he asked, getting to the reason for my call.

121

"What's the starting pay for new graduates?"

"According to NIH guidelines, any post-doctoral positions funded by NIH should have a base salary of $42 thousand," he said, "How much did you think it would be?"

"Most of what I've heard is around that amount but I thought it would have been at least around $60 thousand."

"It should be with the education and skills that you have to bring to the table but unfortunately it's not. Have you got an offer?" he asked.

"Not officially, I'm going over to UNC for an interview next week."

"Good luck on that and don't be a stranger I want to see you at my wedding," he said.

"Thank you and I'll do that," I said, telling him a bald-faced lie, there was no way I was going to another wedding any time soon unless it was my own.

I made one more call to Jasmine. I needed to get some perspective on a few things. I was getting discouraged and I needed her to tell me what it looked like through her rose-colored glasses. Not only was I pissed at the small amount of money that I would be making but Jeff had found somebody before I did. Obviously it must be easier for men to find someone to love and commit to them than it was for women and looks don't even make a difference.

"Hello, Tia, I'm ready for the good news," Jasmine said, recognizing my number.

"First I need you to pull me back from the edge again," I said, feeling down.

"What is it now, Dr. King," she asked with the anticipation going out of her voice.

"I got the call from UNC today about my itinerary and the salary for the position. I can't believe I went through eleven years of college to make $41 thousand."

"Welcome to my world, baby," Jasmine said. "I know it's not as much as you deserve but there are quite a few others who don't even make that much money. The paltry pay they give to people in academia should be scandalous. That's why I went into administration for my doctorate instead of science, but I still can't catch a break. That's what time it is. Take this opportunity and run with it, it will put you on a path where you can keep moving forward."

"I will, I just needed to vent for a minute," I said.

"That's what I'm here for; people come in here venting all day long."

"I'm not finished," I said, taking a breath. "Do you remember that big boy named Jeff who was always trying to get with me, the one who got the job at NIH?"

"Yeah, he was crazy about you."

"I called him to see why the money for post-docs is so short and he dropped a bomb on me. He's engaged and the wedding is before the year is out. I'm so tired of everybody I went to school with getting on the train and going on with their lives, getting good jobs, getting married and all I get to do is watch them pass me by. I want to ride too, shit. When will I have a chance to get on the damn train? What do I have to do?"

"Calm yourself down, you've had a few chances already to get on the love train and you chose to wait. I've told you that the perfect man for you might not look the way you think he should. Stop crossing people off the list before you give them a chance."

"I've told you, I'm not going to settle, Jasmine."

"Okay, that's fine. Anyway things are moving much better for you now on the job front, you've got an excellent chance to be employed before the month is out."

"I have to concentrate on that for now, but it seems like I'm always getting the short end of the stick," I said, still feeling sorry for myself.

"Are you talking about Reggie again," Jasmine teased.

I had to laugh, "That's why I always call you because you always have me laughing before I get off the phone."

"They say we laugh to keep from crying and that's gospel, girl."

Chapter One

8

Chapter Eight

The week had gone by quickly and I was worried about leaving my mama, her memory was obviously getting worse. I had read that brain stimuli could slow the progress of the disease so I bought her some word search, crosswords, and Sudoku books for some mental exercise.

"Mama I bought you some game books to work on. They say that it helps the memory if you get your mind working," I said, handing her the Sudoku book.

"I don't like numbers. It will frustrate me more than stimulate me."

"What about the crosswords, and the word search books aren't that hard. I bought them in large print so you won't have to strain your eyes."

"I occupy my time the way I want to, I like watching my shows on TV," she said, getting agitated with me.

"You could at least watch *Wheel of Fortune* or *Jeopardy* every now and then, they would at least give you something to think about."

"I can still decide what I want to watch on TV if you don't mind," she said, staring me down and letting me know I had worn out my welcome for the moment.

This woman was dependent on me for so many of her needs right now but she still wouldn't listen to a word I said. The reality of what Dr. Burton said about her eventually having to be placed in a facility was rearing its ugly head. I went back to my room to pack my bag for my trip to North Carolina.

The morning of my flight I was caught in a whirlwind of emotions. I was apprehensive about leaving my mama for three days, but Thomas and my daddy were going to work together and see that she was taken care of. I have to admit that I need a break from being caretaker for a minute. I'm excited and nervous about meeting Dr. Hartman and his crew.

"I'm leaving now, Mama, my phone is on, call me, and I'll call you," I said as I gave her a goodbye hug and kiss in the living room.

"All right, baby, have a good time and I'll see you when you get back," she said, turning her attention back to the TV.

This was crazy. I was off to a job interview in another state and I wasn't even sure that I could take it if they offered it to me. I was losing my mama a little more every day. I stopped myself in mid-thought and refused to think about it anymore. I had to have a future and a life of my own, any other decisions aside from that would have to wait. I closed the door behind me.

***

"Now this is the way to travel," I said, pulling my car into the airport long-term parking under the noise of a plane in take-off. I'm Dr. Tia King, going on an all expense paid interview in North Carolina where my flight, accommodations, and meals will be paid for by my hopefully soon-to-be employer. On the plane I found the window seat designated for me, slid in and buckled up. It may be coach but it feels like first class to me. The flight isn't full and the seat next to me is empty and that means I don't have to rub hips with a total stranger for an hour.

"Would you like something to drink?" the stewardess asked when we reach altitude.

"I'll have a Coke please," I said, reaching for the small pack of nuts she was handing out.

Sipping on the drink and gazing out the window between the clouds and seeing the ground far below I thank God that I'm back to living again and not merely existing for others. I needed this confirmation that somebody else in the world knows I'm here and that I'm a valuable person. I pray that this plane is the vehicle that takes me closer to my purpose. My deep contemplation is interrupted by the captain instructing us to raise our seats back up and replace the trays to prepare for landing.

I get off the plane and make my way to the escalator leading to baggage claim. On the way down I see there is a young lady holding up my name on a card. I've seen this in the movies and suddenly I feel like an important dignitary coming to town. I get to the bottom of the stairs and I can see her still looking up in the flow of people coming down.

I walk over beside her and said, "Hello, I'm Tia King."

"Hello," she said awkwardly, "I didn't realize you had come down already, I'm sorry I didn't see you."

"It's all right, we've never met so I didn't expect you to recognize me and pick me out of a crowd," I said, joking to help her relax. "That's what the sign is for."

"That's true, welcome. I'm Jennifer and I'm going to get you settled in your hotel and bring you over to a reception we're having for all the post-doc candidates."

"Nice to meet you, Jennifer, that sounds like fun," I said, walking over to the spinning conveyor belt to retrieve my luggage.

I could feel her eyes on my back while I lifted my bag into the trunk of her car. Typical response from the young white students when they meet an over thirty, heavyset black woman, with all the qualifications that they are trying to get.

I turned around and met her stare and she said, "Your presentation is scheduled for 2:00 tomorrow if that's agreeable to you."

"Absolutely, that's fine," I said, going around to the car door.

"Two of the other candidates did their seminar earlier today and we'll have three tomorrow."

We drove in silence to the Embassy Suites and I enjoyed the sights of the city on the way. I got checked in and Jennifer accompanied me to the room.

Riding the elevator up to my floor I asked, "Do I need to change into something nicer?"

"No, it's casual, your jeans are fine."

She stayed on her feet waiting at the door hinting that we didn't have a lot of time. I put my bag on the bed in the bedroom and pulled out my smaller bag of toiletries. I quickly brushed my teeth, washed my face, combed my hair, and freshened up my make-up. I took an extra minute and changed my blouse to get the road dust off, I believed in being prepared just in case Mr. Right was attending the reception.

"Let's do it, Jennifer," I said, opening the hotel room door and feeling my anticipation building again.

The campus was very attractive. Most of them are with all the greenery and landscaping painstakingly kept up on a daily basis. Inside the door of the reception room there was a greeting table where I was given a name tag. I looked around the room and it was typical for most science meetings, there were only two other black faces, a total switch from the culture and environment at TSU. I sighed at the odds of meeting an attractive specimen in this place. Scanning across the faces I was met with several smiles although none were welcoming. I determined that this was going to be all business. It was time to fall into the group and mix until I found someone friendly who I could make eye contact with during my presentation.

I walked over to the drink station and got a glass of Pepsi and headed over to the posters that were exhibited in the reception. I walked up to a young man who looked like a straight-up science geek with his horn-rimmed glasses and curly hair standing by one of the posters.

"Hello," I said as I move closer to read his title, "Is this your work?"

"Yes it is," he answered, "I'm Daniel, a third year grad student here. You must be one of the post-doc candidates coming into the department."

"Is it that obvious?" I asked, trying to make a joke.

"Yeah it is," he answered, totally serious and I could sense some underlying issues.

Since he was keeping it real I decided to ask the questions that had filled my head as soon as I walked in the door.

"Are there any black faculty or post-docs in the department, I don't see many in the room?"

"No, we don't have any black faculty or post-docs but we do have two black students," he said, speaking as if he had a problem with the diversity in the department.

Wanting to know what the real deal was and if this would be a good move for me, I asked, "From one recent graduate student to another, what do you think about the department and does it support the research efforts of post-docs and junior faculty?"

"If you can get inside the special loop here, its smooth sailing in beautiful waters," he said in a low voice, "If you don't, it's a hell storm that you fight every day."

"That's pretty scary," I said, thinking that I had already experienced my share of hell in getting my degree."

"You don't look like you scare easily," he said, looking me in the eye.

"I don't, but I don't walk past danger signs either."

"Tia, come and join us," Dr. Hartman said, putting his arm around my shoulder and guiding me to the center of the floor, "There are some other folks I'd like you to meet."

"I'd love to," I said, putting on my happy to meet you smile.

"I'd like to introduce you all to Dr. Tia King," Dr. Hartman said, breaking into the circle, "She is one of our guest candidates for the post-doc positions and you will hear from her tomorrow at her presentation at 2:00."

"Hello," an older woman, who I assumed was faculty, said as she extended her hand out to me, "I'm Rebecca and I'm looking forward to hearing about your research."

"It's good to be here. From what I've seen of the campus grounds it's very nice," I said, following her eyes as she looked me up and down.

"I hope Steve told you this is a relaxed gathering where we can get to know more about you," she said before the interrogation began. "Are you originally from Tennessee?"

"Yes I am, I've lived there all my life."

"Really," she added, "Have you traveled much?"

"Not as of yet, it seems like I've been in school most of my life but I'm hoping that I will be able to do more now that I have the terminal degree," I said with a smile.

"What do you like to do in your spare time?" Steve asked.

"I love going to the movies and trying new restaurants."

"Oh really," one of the younger attractive women in the circle said, "What kinds of restaurants and food do you like?"

This one was a mean girl and I could tell she was looking for a spot to stick her knife in. I'm sure she was anxious to hear about my love for soul food, especially fried chicken, turnip greens, and watermelon but I refused to give her the satisfaction. This must be the loop that Daniel was talking about.

"My taste buds are eclectic, I don't have a real favorite," I said.

"I can understand that, there are so many ethnic varieties now," she said with her knife finding its mark in my behind.

I can't believe it, a pain in the ass and I've only been here for 30 minutes. Who is this chick?

"I didn't catch your name, are you faculty or staff?" I asked her, preparing myself for a mental battle if that's what she wanted.

"Brittany, I'm a visiting candidate also," she answered, "I

presented my research presentation earlier today."

"I'm sorry I missed it," I said, looking at the ceiling, "I'm sure it was quite informative."

"Yes, she and Skip Manning did a good job today, you and the other guys will be tomorrow," Steve interjected.

So that's why her claws were out, she was attacking the other female candidate. In all fairness they should pick one female out of the three and she wanted to start her campaign to increase her chances. There was no way I was going to let her get into my head before I presented, I didn't need the distraction. I didn't know if this was the ideal place for me but it was the only one that had invited me so far.

"Excuse me, I going to check out the buffet, it was nice meeting you all and I'm sure we'll talk some more," I said with a smile before I cut my eye at Brittany.

It never fails; there is always a fly in the room buzzing around getting on my nerves. So be it, I was invited here just like the rest of them on the basis of my accomplishments and none of them were better than I am. Besides, the layout of the food was spectacular, they had everything from barbecue to Mexican and then to sushi. I made myself a hefty plate and found a comfortable seat near the drink station to eat. If my life was a movie, my Curtis Mayfield theme song would be coming in from the background, because I'm a winner.

Scoping out the room from the supreme vantage point, I could see that there were small groups of two or three and the rest were centered around Dr. Hartman. That's the circle I need to penetrate to secure myself one of these positions. I savored the last bite of an enchilada and went over to break the chain.

"I feel much better," I said, "I hadn't eaten all day."

I heard a sniggle from Brittany, the nasty fly, but I ignored it.

"Can I get you a glass of wine or a beer?" Steve asked.

"No, thank you, I don't drink," I said casually.

From the looks in the circle I knew I had violated one of their cardinal rules and it was too late to pull the words back into my mouth.

Jasmine always tells me to just take the drink and nurse it because some people are uncomfortable around others who don't drink, they feel judged.

"I prefer to eat my extra calories," I said, laughing. Self-deprecating humor always breaks the tension in a room, it makes others feel better about themselves. "I do however make exceptions for New Year's, weddings, graduations, and birthday celebrations."

Steve let out a big laugh, "Yes, that was a good one; there are exceptions to every rule. I'll have to remember that one, but I'll need to add football and hockey games, grant award letters, and Saturday nights."

I listened to a few more bad jokes before I said, "I'm going to have to call it an evening, I don't want to yawn all through my talk tomorrow."

"We understand, we've all stood in front of a firing squad," Rebecca said, patting me on the shoulder. "It will be quick and painless, I promise."

Another burst of laughter went around the circle and then I added, "I could always prolong the agony with an extended version of my presentation."

"I love a girl who doesn't come to a fight empty-handed," Steve said, raising his glass. "Have a good night, Tia. Jennifer will get you back to your hotel."

Daniel walked up to me as I looked around the room for my ride.

"It looked like you held your head above the water," he said.

"For now, but I get the feeling it's going to be rough sailing tomorrow," I said, spotting Jennifer near the exit door. "Will you be there?"

"I hadn't planned on it but I think I will."

"I'll see you in the afternoon then," I said, knowing he would have the friendly eyes there for me to talk to.

"I don't mean to be a killjoy, but would you mind giving me a ride back to the hotel?" I asked Jennifer, interrupting her conversation with some other students.

"Don't worry about it, I'm here at your disposal, and they are paying me well," she said good-humoredly.

"That's good, now I don't feel so bad."

Traffic was much lighter now that it was in the late evening and we got to the hotel in less than ten minutes. I was exhausted, it had been a long day.

"Thank you, Jennifer, I appreciate you chauffeuring me around today," I said as I climbed out of the car.

"What time would you like me to come for you tomorrow?" she asked.

"I think I'll pass on attending the other seminars so I'll be ready about 1:00," I replied before I closed the car door.

Inside the hotel, I couldn't wait for the elevator to reach my floor. I slid the card into the slot on the door, when the green light turned on I pushed it open and put the 'do not disturb' sign on the outside. I kicked off my shoes, walked back to the bathroom, and turned on the shower. I stood under the hot streams of water praying that all the frustrations of the evening were washed down the drain.

I thought about the reception I just attended. Was this my goal? Was this what I had worked so hard for, to play politics and mind games with a bunch of people I didn't even like? By the time I was fresh and clean I had reminded myself that this was just a job, not a lifelong commitment. It was the start of my career and I could learn a lot from them here, besides the contract was only for one year. I crawled between the crisp white sheets and fell asleep.

I got up early, put on some sweats, and took a walk around the grounds of the hotel to calm the morning jitters that had returned. I stopped in the lobby for the hot breakfast that they were serving. I sat down at a table by myself and ate some pancakes and an omelet made to order. I eased back over to the serving area to get some fruit, donuts, and coffee to take to my room for a mid-morning snack. I hated to give presentations on a full stomach. With all the nervousness my digestion slows down and it makes me burp.

Back in the room I picked up my cell phone to check on my mama.

"Good morning, Mama," I said when she answered, "How are you? Are Daddy and Thomas taking care of you?"

"Yeah I'm good, Tia, how are you doing, baby?"

"So far so good, Mama, I give my talk today."

"That's good, baby, did you study last night."

"No I didn't, I just came back to the room after the reception and went to bed. I've been through it all before. I should know it like the back of my hand."

"Okay, baby, well good luck on your test. I'll talk to you later.

It just occurred to me at that moment how short our conversations had become. We used to talk on and on about everything, now she only gave me short answers. She didn't ask me any questions or tease me about being desperate. "Help me Lord," I said to myself. It was hard to know my mama's mind was drifting more every day. What could I do to help her if I didn't get on my own two feet? I turned on my laptop for one last run-through of my power-point before I put my feet up on the sofa for a short power nap. When I woke up, I reached for my phone.

"I need a game plan, coach," I said to Jasmine after she picked up.

"Honey, that's all any of us need. What's up?"

"I'm trying to decide what to wear to give my talk."

"How old was the department head?" Jasmine asked.

"She seemed around 60 years old, give or take a few years."

"What was she wearing?"

"They were all casual, she had on jeans like everybody else."

"They sound like an informal group. You could wear some jeans, a dress shirt and a blazer."

"I only brought one pair and I had them on all day yesterday."

"Well, I wouldn't wear a dress; you don't want to appear too conservative or standoffish."

"The only thing I have left to wear is my black slacks and a shell shirt."

"That'll work, put your blazer on so your booty won't steal

the show and you'll be fine. Go out there and show them who you are. The worst thing that can happen is you don't get the position, and you can't miss what you never had."

"That would be debatable but I don't have time right now, I'll call you when I get back home."

I clicked the YouTube icon on my laptop and typed in Curtis Mayfield's "We're a Winner" to play while I got dressed. I put on my light version of make-up, sprayed my understated perfume, and I was ready to go.

My phone rang at 1:00 on the nose. Jennifer was downstairs waiting out front to take me back to the campus. I took one last look in the mirror, grabbed my jump drive, gulped down my coffee, and headed out the door to the elevator. In the car ride I replayed the conversation I had with Jasmine in my mind, this wasn't life or death, it was a presentation of my work.

"Our seminars are held in Life Sciences Hall across from the research labs," Jennifer said, leading the way, "We'll take a tour there after you're finished."

I nodded my head as we walked into the lobby of the Hall. I noticed a sign that pointed to the theater area.

"The presentations of the candidates have been held in the smaller theater around the corner to the left. You have about thirty minutes, you can set up whenever you want," Jennifer said, standing back. "I'll be back before you're done."

"Thank you again," I said, turning and walking to the smaller theater.

I saw a sign above the double doors that said "Comfort Hall." Inside I could understand why, it was an intimate theater that seated less than fifty people. The walls were painted a pale blue like the sky and the carpet was dense, and colored in neutral beige, it was like walking across the sand on a beach. The cushioned seats were covered in colorful geometric pattern with matching armrests. This is first class I thought as I went over to the podium and turned on the overhead. No log-on was needed, so I put in my jump drive and clicked computer. I was ready.

I went back outside to wait for my grand entrance. I had discovered years back when I had to review articles for journal club that I was more nervous when I sat and watched everybody arrive one by one versus when I came in after they were all seated. I had about fifteen minutes to kill before show time so I sat down on a wall to watch the students as they paraded across the campus. A squirrel scampered up close to me and looked me in the face demanding some token of generosity.

"I don't have anything, my friend," I said, staring back.

He responded with a quick twitch of his head and for a second I thought he was about to attack. Typical, just because you're heavy, folks think you always have snacks on you. I checked my watch and I had four minutes to spare. I headed back to the small theater and entered the room with perfect timing.

"Good afternoon ladies and gentlemen," Steve said, beginning his introduction, "We are happy to welcome, Dr. Tia King, to our university as a post-doctoral research fellow candidate. She is a graduate of Tennessee State University and will be presenting her research on the c-myc gene. Join me in giving her a warm reception of applause."

They had already read it and that's why I was invited here.

They just wanted to see me jump through their hoops. We were past qualifications, all of us were qualified, this was the popularity portion of the pageant and I couldn't be anything else but who I am. There weren't any black judges, yet these were supposed to be my peers. What could I say, nothing to do but to do it.

I moved to the podium, clicked start-show for my power-point and began, "I want to thank Dr. Hartman and the Department of Molecular Biology for this opportunity to speak with you and share my research. The title for this presentation is, "Stopping the C-Myc Gene in its Tracks," which was the basis for the question that preceded this research."

I went through my introduction, the objectives of my research, the background literature, the data, and the conclusions. I finished in twenty-seven minutes, close to the thirty minutes that Jasmine had advised me to stick near.

"With all of that said, are there any questions?" I asked calmly and confident now that I had completed my presentation.

There were a quite a few questions, although none that I hadn't heard before in my committee meetings or at my defense. I hadn't met but a few of the people who were asking them, so I wasn't sure who was gunning for me, but it didn't matter. I noticed Daniel sitting in the back with a satisfied smile. There were a lot of things that I wasn't sure of in my life but this I had down to a science, pun intended.

"Thank you, Dr. King, for gracing us with an interesting and informative presentation," Steve said, joining me at the podium.

There was some brief applause before the group began to file out of the theater.

"Good job, Tia, that was impressive," Steve said, putting his arm around my shoulders. "Now there will be a tour of our research facility before we go to a dinner for our candidates."

"That sounds good to me," I said before he moved to the front to lead the tour.

The rest of the day was a blur of tours, meeting more people, and eating. By the time Jennifer dropped me off in the front of Embassy Suites that night, I was as spent as a one dollar bill in Mexico. I threw my feet up on the coffee table as soon as I sat down and I swear that in the quiet I could almost hear them throbbing.

I turned on the TV and zoned out on reruns of the Martin Show. When I woke up it was 2:00 in the morning. I had an early flight at 10:45 so I set the alarm clock to wake me at 7:00. There was no sense coming to this hotel and not having breakfast everyday that you're here. I got out of my clothes and threw on a night gown and fell into the bed.

Jennifer was there at 8:30 to get me to the airport and I was ready and waiting in the lobby with a full tummy and my luggage at my side.

"Thank you so much for all your assistance," I said, shaking her hand before I headed down to airport security. "You have been pleasant as well as efficient."

"You're welcome; I've had much more demanding people to work with so it was no problem," she said, "Good luck on getting the fellowship."

I waved goodbye unsure of whether I would be back. When I got through security and had my shoes back on I found a seat away from the clusters of waiting passengers to wait for the plane to board. I pulled out my phone to check my messages and it was full. I had let them pile up not wanting to think about anything but getting through my talk.

All of my girls had texted me words of encouragement, but I was surprised to see that Reggie had practically blown my phone up. There were three voicemails and four text messages from him. I hadn't talked to him in over a month and since I was trying to watch my weight and had sworn off fast food there wasn't much incentive to connect. He probably didn't have much more to offer since the last time I saw him.

9

Chapter Nine

The plane ride back was booked tight. I ended up with an aisle seat next to a mean version of Betty White who smelled like she had taken a bath in Elizabeth Taylor's White Diamonds. She gave me the evil eye when I brushed against her as I fastened my seatbelt. I leaned back and closed my eyes to block out my surroundings but every time somebody walked by they bumped or brushed against the part of my hip that was sticking out from under my armrest and brought me back. By the time we landed in Nashville I was positive that I had a black and blue bruise on my leg to take home as a memento.

I opened the back door at the house and when I heard the television playing I knew I was back at home. I eased through the kitchen to my room not ready to face my real world yet. I put my bag down on the floor and fell across the bed. I laid there until I heard my daddy call me.

"Tia, are you home?"

"Yeah, Daddy, I'm back," I said, coming out of my room to the kitchen to talk.

"That's right on time, baby, I've got some things to do before I go to work and I haven't made your mama's lunch yet."

"I got it don't worry," I said while he grabbed his jacket from the back of one of the chairs.

"How did your interview go, did they offer you the job?"

"It went well but I have to wait to hear their decision."

"Don't sweat it, baby, they'll call you," he said, giving me a kiss on the check on his way out the back door.

"Aren't you going to say goodbye to Mama?" I yelled behind him.

"She don't pay me no mind, I'll see you later," he said, closing the door.

I could feel what he was saying, Mama was slowly withdrawing from us into her world of TV land. She hadn't called me once the whole time I had been gone and it was just six months ago that she would call me at least three times a day. I walked slowly into the living room hoping that my mama would be there in mind as well as body.

"Hey, Mama," I said, walking over to give her a hug. "Did Daddy and Thomas take good care of you while I was gone?"

"Tia, I am a grown woman and I run this house," she said, pushing me away, "I don't need nobody to take care of me."

"I know that, Mama, you know what I mean. It's hard for you to stand on your feet for a long time."

"You all sure do get on my nerves fussing over me. If y'all would leave me alone I'd be fine."

"Do you want to hear about my trip, Mama?" I asked, trying to get her attention away from the TV.

"Not right now, baby, you can tell me about it later."

I couldn't wait to get out of the room, this was too weird for words, my mama always wanted to hear every detail of whatever I was doing ever since I was in the first grade. This wasn't just about her memory, she was becoming a different person. I called Dr. Burton's office to leave a message for him to call me.

"Hello," I said, holding my breath when I answered the house landline. This must be the last phone in America that doesn't have caller ID.

"Hello, this is Dr. Burton, I'm returning a call to Tia King," the familiar voice said on the other line.

"Hi, Dr. Burton, I was calling because I've noticed some more changes in my mother. It's not just the fact that her short term memory is compromised, it's that her personality and her interests seem to be changing. She doesn't want to do much else besides watch the TV."

"That is not unusual behavior, Ms. King. So many of my patients have changes in their disposition, it's part of the progression of the disease. There's nothing for you to be worried about, but you and your family must begin to mentally prepare yourselves for the changes and the need for increased care for your mother."

"Is there anything we can do to slow down the process?" I asked him.

"Unfortunately not, Miss King, the period of deterioration varies with each patient, although she may benefit from increased mental stimulation."

"Thank you, Dr. Burton," I said before I hung up.

I hadn't been home a good day and already I felt like the walls were closing in and I didn't have the freedom to escape, I was trapped. I checked my cell phone for messages hoping there would be one that offered me solutions to my problems. Among the long list of text messages, there was one from Jasmine reminding me to call her when I got back in town. I dialed her number and listened to the rings that were my lifeline to the outside world.

"Dr. King, what's up girl?" she said cheerfully.

"I just got back and I need to get away," I said, trying to joke, "I'm really tripping."

"What's going on?" She asked. "Was your mother okay when you got back?"

"Yeah, she was fine physically but she acts like that TV in there is her husband, daughter, and her best friend. She doesn't talk to me or even seem grateful that I'm here."

"Yeah you are tripping, Tia, your mother is sick and she can't help you because she's struggling to help herself. You have to be patient with her and take this time with her as a blessing."

"I know that but it scares me. I keep thinking that if I get an offer I won't even be able to leave."

"What are your feelings about how everything went at UNC?"

"I don't know, I didn't get a strong vibe on what they thought about me."

"You did your part and the odds are in your favor, I wouldn't stress it. If you weren't being highly considered they would not have flown you over there."

"How can I not be stressed with my mom losing it and the fact that I am 34 years old and I can't pay my car insurance or cell phone bill?"

"Girlfriend, when you get yourself employed that situation

will be worked out. You need to chill out, you're getting overly frustrated. You are going to have to learn how to crack open a bottle of wine, kick back and relax."

"This is not the right time for me to start drinking, believe me," I said with a laugh, "Then there would be two people in here losing their minds."

"Well, at least I feel better," Jasmine said, "If you can still laugh about it you are nowhere near the point of falling off the edge."

"I hope you're right because if you're not, it's not going to be good. Anyway, I'll talk to you later I've got to go to the store and get something to cook for dinner."

"Take care, girl, buy a lotto ticket while you're in there, your life can change any day."

"Bye, Jazz, I can always count on you to have on your rose colored glasses."

"I know that's right and I'm not taking them off," she said before she hung up.

***

Two weeks passed and I hadn't got a call or letter from UNC. What was taking them so long to make a decision? I have literally been attached to my cell phone 24/7 trying not to miss any of my calls. I even sleep with it. The only time it's not on me is when I'm in the shower, then it's on the edge of the tub where I can still grab it if it rings. I have asked all my friends how long was a reasonable time to wait before I call UNC back and the consensus was two weeks. Today was the day I had designated for my call back but I was getting scared. I prayed that no news was still good news.

I dialed Kathryn Houston's number, the department administrator, and held my breath until she answered. The holidays were coming and starting a new job would be the best Christmas present I could ask for.

"Hello, this is Tia King; I was one of the post-doc candidates that visited the campus a couple of weeks ago."

"Yes, Dr. King, what can I do for you?" she asked, pretending she wasn't aware of the reason for my call.

"I was curious as to whether a decision had been made on the fellowships," I said, trying to sound casual.

"Yes, the selections have been notified by letter."

It was hard to hold back the barrage of curse words that were rising in my throat. What in the hell was that bullshit supposed to mean. That didn't tell me anything. I pushed further.

"Should I assume that if I haven't received a letter by today that I was not chosen for one of the fellowships?" I asked, trying to maintain the 'it's not that serious' tone in my voice.

"That would probably be correct," she answered and then went silent.

"All right, well I guess there's not much left to say except I think it would have been more professional to notify all the candidates either way. They could be waiting for the decision before they committed to other opportunities," I explained.

"I'm sorry about that, Dr. King," she said, "I will give your suggestion to Dr. Hartman. Is there anything else I can do for you?"

"No, that was all, thank you," I said a few seconds before I heard the line disconnect.

That hurt real bad, my heart sank down to my feet and

they felt like they couldn't hold me up. I sat down on the bed
devastated. I had given the best I had to give and once again
it was thrown back in my face. They didn't even bother to call
me and let me know. Christmas wasn't coming to the King
household this year. I was too embarrassed to tell anybody.
I lay across my bed feeling down, alone, and rejected. The
only person checking for me was Reggie. I broke my promise
to myself and called him. I needed somebody to talk to who
didn't know about my trip.

"Tia, it's about time, I've been blowing up your phone for a
couple of months. What you did was lowdown, you didn't have
to treat a brotha like that."

"I had a lot going on, you know my mother is sick."

"I hear you, that's rough, but I want to see you again.
Everything wasn't the way I wanted when we were together
and I want to make it up to you."

"You need to, because you know that you were really foul
last time."

"I like you, Tia, I think you are a very special lady and I want
our friendship to grow."

It was like food for a child starving in the Third World,
his words lifted my spirits even though I didn't believe half
of them. Sometimes a woman needs to hear certain things,
especially the sweet talk of a man trying to get some, it was
definitely food for thought.

"Everybody deserves a second chance, so I'll give you
that, but I want you to know that I have trust issues. I've had
some men in my life lie to me about having a wife or other
women that they were dealing with. I need to know if you

are truly separated and if you are seeing anyone else right now."

"No, I'm not seeing anybody else. Why would I be trying so hard to get in touch with you if I had someone else?"

"I don't know but it has happened to me in the past and I don't want to be in that situation again," I said in as serious voice as I could muster.

"Come on, Tia, for real. You know I was crazy about you from the first time I saw you."

"Time will tell, I've heard that line before."

"So when can I see you?" he asked, changing his voice and tone. "When are you going to be back in the big city?"

"I still don't have any income to travel back and forth to Nashville so I don't know when that might be."

"I can come and pick you up and drive you back," he said, "It'll give me a chance to meet your family."

"Well if you're coming here then it's up to you, my schedule is wide open."

"That's all I wanted to know. For the holidays I'm pretty much on lockdown with my kids and my parents but after that it'll be me and you."

"Dude, that's next year, I'll believe it when I see it," I said before I hung up the phone.

I kept a low profile for the next week, not answering my phone or text messages. My life was starting to depress me. Thanksgiving went by and even though Christmas was two weeks away I hadn't thought about putting a tree up and I didn't even have money to buy my nieces and nephews any gifts. I didn't want to talk to anybody until I had some good news to tell them, specifically that I had gotten a job.

I updated my application for the University of Phoenix and to my surprise they sent me an e-mail the next day. They needed three recommendations in order to process my application. Now I had no choice but to come out of the exile I had sentenced myself to. I was sure to get another dose of humility when I had to ask for recommendations from people I didn't want to know I hadn't found a position yet. The first call was to Jasmine.

"Merry Christmas to you too," she said when she answered.

"Jazz, you don't have to tell me, I know I have been extra," I said, trying to head off her giving me an earful.

"You got that right. What's the problem? You've been ignoring everybody, I was about to drive down to that teeny tiny town and turn it out."

"UNC didn't choose me and not only that, they didn't even have the courtesy to notify me. I had to call the office to find out. That was a low blow and I've been depressed and feeling sorry for myself. I didn't feel like letting folks know that I had been passed over."

"I'm sorry to hear that. I know you had high expectations for yourself but now you know that you live in the same world that the rest of us have to contend with. People judge us all the time based on a ton of reasons, race, color, looks, weight, status, and there's nothing we can do about it. They make decisions on whether they will hire us, fire us, and even marry us because of them. That's the real fact of life and we've all been through it."

"That's true and I'm sorry about that," I sighed. "I do not want to live like this. I want to be judged according to who I am and what I have to offer."

"Unfortunately, you are Tia King and that is Martin Luther King's dream, and it's still not a reality. Nevertheless we have to keep striving with the hope that every now and then things will go our way."

"I'd rather have the money I need. It's more important for me to be able to handle my business than to have these so-called accomplishments."

"Girl, you are down but you're not out. That wasn't the last job on earth, there's at least one left for you somewhere."

"I'm not giving up. I just got an e-mail from the University of Phoenix asking me for three recommendations. The thing is I don't know who I can ask?"

"You know you can count on me for one, now you only need two more."

"Thanks, Jazz, I need some help. You won't believe how low I've sunk."

"What do you mean?" She asked curiously, in a lower tone.

"I called Reggie today," I said hesitantly.

"Are you serious?" she asked, waiting for the punch line.

"I am, my confidence was way down and I was having a weak moment."

"I'm not going to touch that."

"He said he's coming to pick me up and bring me to Nashville in about a week."

"Like I said, I'm going to leave my jury out of this one until I get some more evidence. I don't want to be too quick to judge. I thought he was a good dude when I first met him, maybe he was having an off weekend."

"I hope so because I need to get my groove on, you know I'm

not one to do without."

"My lips will remain sealed, I don't want to take your mama's place and mention the word desperate."

"You always say that ten years ago there may have been a reason to save it, now is the time to do me. Just because I don't have a husband doesn't mean I don't have needs."

"Go on, hot stuff, handle your business, I'll have the letter for you in a couple of days."

"They have something online that they want you to fill out, I'll send you the website and the code number to enter."

"Is that how it's done now? Keep me straight, girl."

"Thanks for always being there, it helps."

"That's why I'm here, I'm a friend."

"Bye, Jazz, I've got work to do."

"Don't we all," she added before we both clicked end.

***

The University of Phoenix offered me a teaching position for the spring semester in one of the on-campus science classes. The class met one day a week for three hours. I could drive up for my class and get back home to take care of Mama without any trouble. The main drawback was that they only paid me $1500 for teaching one class in the semester. Yet, for me it wasn't about the money at this point, it was about the self-respect that I needed from working.

There was a dress code for professors so I slid into my go-to black slacks and top with a blazer to wear on the first day of my class.

"Mama, I'm going to be out for a while teaching a class. I've made your lunch and something sweet for you to snack on. I'll be back as soon as I can."

"Go on, Tia, I don't know why you're always treating me like I need a babysitter, I was taking care of myself before your smart ass was born."

"Take a deep breath and ignore the comment, she's not herself," I said silently.

My mama has always had a mouth on her, but she rarely used it on me. Now that I wasn't getting that special treatment I was starting to feel resentful. I grabbed my messenger bag with my some-timey laptop in it and the textbook that had been sent to me and went out the door to perform my first official job since I graduated over a year ago. I reached Nashville about an hour later.

"Good afternoon class, my name is Dr. Tia King," I said after I located my classroom. I looked over the uninterested faces that filled the classroom while I handed out the syllabus that the college had provided, "I will be you Biology 101 professor this semester."

"Hello, Doctor, I'm ready to make an easy 'A'," one rude boy in the back yelled out, designating himself as the class clown.

"That's up to you and the effort you give to your studies," I replied without looking at him. "The first thing I would like for us to do is go around the room and get everyone to introduce themselves. Tell us your name, your major, and your long-term goal. We'll start at the front on the left, go down the aisle and move towards the right."

"My name is Jayla Jamison, I haven't chosen a major yet but I hope to be an actress," the cute girl in the front replied.

Behind her a long lanky young man said, "My name is DeQuan Miller and I'm a business major, I'm going to need to learn how to manage all my money when I get to the NBA."

The introductions didn't get much better as they moved down and across the room. I had a class full of space cadets that I had to teach the basics of biology, however, I was never one to shrink from a challenge. An hour and a half into the class I let them take a twenty minute break for the restroom or the cafeteria. We reconvened and I hadn't been lecturing for ten minutes before they started nagging me about dismissing the class early. I'm sure this was payback for some of my behavior during my undergrad years. I ignored their pleas until we were fifteen minutes before the class was scheduled to end and then I relented.

"That concludes our first class, the reading assignment and questions to be answered are indicated on the syllabus, I hope to see you all again next week."

I felt good, I was a professor. I had taught my first class. I reached in my bag for my phone and called Reggie.

"What's going on?" he said, sounding surprised to hear from me.

"I just got done teaching my first class," I said, impressed with myself.

"That's cool, why don't I come and pick you up this weekend and we can celebrate your new job?" he suggested, sounding excited for me.

"Are you sure you're ready to meet my family?"

"Absolutely, I've told you that you mean a lot to me."

"I've heard that before, you're going to have to show me something," I said, and I could feel my confidence coming back.

"I'll show you something," he said in a cocky tone before he hung up.

I laughed to myself because he must have forgotten that I had already seen his stuff and he needed to bring more than that to the table to turn me on. I had a piece of a job but I wanted a whole man to have a relationship with. I wanted to get married. Most women say you can't get all the things you need from one man and now I'm a believer. A lot of men may say that they can't get everything that they need from one woman, but the difference is a woman will try her ass off to be all things to everybody.

10

Chapter Ten

My life seemed to be taking a turn for the better. I was working and Reggie had called and promised that he would be coming to town on Friday night to take me to Nashville for a nice weekend. The only worry I had at the moment was how to introduce him to my mama.

Mama was always hard on any guy that I had introduced her to from the time I started bringing them home. I don't know if it was about what went down between her and my daddy years ago or if maybe it was due to someone before he came on the scene but she has some bitterness to men. They are all ugly and look like some type of animal that she never fails to describe. Since the beginning of her problems with Alzheimer's she has become even meaner. I don't know what kind of earful she will serve up to Reggie, but I'm sure it won't be pretty. I made a big dinner and baked a cake to soften her up.

"Tia, you put your foot in this macaroni and cheese," she said, enjoying the special meal I had spent three hours cooking.

"Mama, I have a friend coming by this weekend to pick me up," I said casually between bites of cornbread, "I'm going to spend the weekend in Nashville."

I said a silent prayer, hoping that her mind was focused on her food and that I could slip this by her without any fanfare.

"What friend?" she asked with her senses sharp, "Coming here, when?"

It was like somebody had turned the light switch on and she could see again. "Chile, I don't know when you're going to stop fooling around with these lowdown niggas, they aren't about anything," she said, holding a forkful of meatloaf in the air.

"You took a chance on somebody, Mama, and I'm going to do the same thing," I said defensively.

"I was young and dumb but I have taught you better."

"Look, I'm not marrying the guy, we're trying to get to know each other," I said, ready to close the subject and unable to celebrate the fact that the mama I knew had resurfaced.

"Is that all you're going to do?" she asked, swallowing my dinner and spitting out sarcasm.

"I'm grown, so what I do is my business," I said respectfully. "He wants to meet my family when he comes but if you don't feel like it, we'll skip it."

"Oh no, I want to meet him too," she said, shaking her head. "They can always fool you, but I can see right through them."

"I hope Daddy will be here too," I said, ignoring her last remark, "He's supposed to be off from work this weekend."

"He needs to try and get some overtime, he's not good for much else," she snapped, dismissing my plans for a nice family gathering.

On Friday afternoon my weekend bag was packed and I was ready to go. I loved my mama and I wanted to take care of her but it wasn't easy. I needed these few days out of the house before the roles were changed and I wanted to beat her butt. I texted our address to Reggie after breakfast and he texted me back that it was in his GPS and he would be on the road by lunchtime. The thought that I would be laying next to another warm body tonight had me all excited. I chalked up our last experience as an awkward first time and the second time around would be all good. I decided to get sexy. I picked out a v-neck sweater that let my cleavage get a taste of the fall air and flat-ironed my hair.

"Your friend is here," Dad yelled back to me when he heard the knock on the door.

"Am I the only one who knows how to answer a door around here?" I asked them as I hurried to the front door dropping my travel bag by the sofa.

"Hello, long time no see," I said, smiling at Reggie, "Come on in."

"You look nice," he said, returning my smile with a wink of his eye.

"My parents are in the living room, I'll introduce you and then we're out."

"Sounds like a plan to me" he said, following close behind me.

"Mama and Daddy, this is Reggie Woods, he's a scientific products salesman, I met him at TSU before I graduated."

"Nice to meet you," Daddy said, shaking his hand.

"It's good to finally meet you both, I wasn't able to come to the graduation," Reggie replied.

Mama stayed quiet wearing a look on her face like she smelled something bad.

"We are going to get back on the road so we can dodge some of the rush hour traffic," I said, putting on my jacket and grabbing my purse and bag.

"Okay, baby," Daddy said, standing up to give me a hug, "Drive careful, Reggie."

"We will," I said, stopping to give Mama a kiss on the cheek but she turned away to look at the TV again.

"That wasn't so bad," Reggie said, taking my bag and tossing it in the trunk of his car.

"My mama is not herself anymore and it hurts," I told him after I swallowed the lump in my throat. "She would never meet a guy I'm dealing with and not say something."

"I'm sorry about that but remember she's still here in one piece. Hold on to what you have and don't take it for granted."

"Thanks for saying that, you earned some bonus points today," I said, feeling better about the situation with him and my mama.

It felt good to be on a road trip with a man there to do the driving. I smiled when I thought that I was half of a couple. I leaned over closer to him savoring the feeling and for the first time I wished that the distance to get to Nashville was longer. We got into town in just over an hour.

"Do you want to get some food or do you want to check into the hotel first?" he asked, slapping me on the thigh.

"I'm hungry, let's get something to eat," I said, patting his hand.

"That's cool, what do you have a taste for?"

"Let me think," I said, wondering why I couldn't make this decision inside the restaurant while I looked at the menu.

"How about some barbecue, chicken, or a burger?" he suggested as we approached downtown.

"I hope you're not thinking about pulling up to some fast food joint again?" I said with a laugh, even though I was dead serious.

"Food is food, Tia, you don't have to spend a lot to get a decent meal," he said, pulling off the interstate on the Broadway exit.

"I'm not going to front," I said, searching for the kindest words in my vocabulary to express myself, "I've eaten my share of fast food and ordered plates out of soul food spots, I still do. I'm just not going to let a man who thinks he's going to get in these panties think he can feed it to me. You have got to do better than that. I have other male friends and I mean just friends who take me out and spend more on me than you do."

"I've told you my situation," he said, getting irritated, "That's the trouble with a lot of women; they say they want to meet a nice guy but then they're stuck on a materialistic tip."

"Before we started hanging out you weren't singing this broke song, you were telling me about all the money you were making in your territory. What went wrong? You didn't have your children yesterday, their expenses are not new."

"Come on, Tia, it's right after the holidays, I've got attorney fees, and I'm trying to spread myself across two households. Let's not go down this road about money and spoil the weekend.

"This not what's up, Reggie. I understand your position. I also think that if going out is too much of a strain on you we might need to hold off until you get it together."

"There's a TGIFriday's over there, is that good enough for you?" he asked in a bad effort to control his attitude.

"I don't have a problem with Friday's, I like their food and the atmosphere," I said, calming down and rubbing his leg. "I think it's a good choice."

He stayed quiet while he pulled into the parking lot with his mad face on. I played it cool, strutted into the restaurant, and waited for him to get over himself. He didn't have anything to say until we were seated in a romantic boot in the back.

"I'm sorry about that scene in the car, I shouldn't have tripped like that. My messed up finances are not your fault," he said, looking at his hands instead of at me, "You deserve the best I have to give."

"That's what I'm talking about," I said, slapping his hands to get his attention, "A few more dollars for a little more class won't break the bank."

"You're right and I'm wrong," he said, joking.

"Go on and preach," I said, teasing him, and the good mood between us was back.

Being the reasonable woman that I am I didn't order an appetizer or dessert and I drank water instead of ordering a Coke to keep the tab to a minimum.

"How do you like teaching?" he asked, changing the subject.

"It's more fun than I thought it would be, my students crack me up. I can't believe they don't know anything about science whatsoever."

"Most people don't," he said, "You've been isolated in a world of academia for so long you forgot about the regular folks."

"How is that possible?" I asked him, "I have never escaped the regular world, I'm still trying to get out of the hood? You're the one who comes from a family with a farm and horses."

"You got me on that," he said. "Are you ready to get out of here?"

"I am, but I have to tell you that I enjoyed the meal and the company," I said, scooting over to get out of the booth.

"Well then, can a brother get a kiss?" he asked when I stood up.

"Public displays of affection are not how I get down," I said, putting on my jacket.

"Then it's time for us to take this to a private place," he said, going into seduction mode.

"I'm ready if you are," I said seductively.

He took my hand and led me out of the Friday's. That was hot, the kind of macho shit that I like. I've always been a big girl so when a man makes me feel like his little woman it's so sexy to me. He opened my car door and helped me get in before he got in. Then he popped in a CD of my man, R. Kelly. Everything was going great until he drove up to the same Days Inn motel that we had stayed in the time before.

Returning to the scene of the crime is never a good move. I was so exasperated that it was my turn to be silent. I couldn't find the words to ask him how many kinds of crazy he was. I don't like motels anyway, but he should have known that this one was played out for us. My fantasy for the evening blew away with the breeze that whipped by me when I got out of the car after he checked in.

"What's got you so quiet all of sudden?" Reggie asked, oblivious to the obvious.

"Nothing, you know I've got a lot on my mind."

"Come on in, I've got the cure for all of it," he said, opening the door to our room.

While he worked up a sweat, I spent most of the night trying to determine if the reason that I wasn't really turned on by him was because of the way he got down or because he never failed to piss me off just before we were about to get to it. He fell asleep after the first round and I wasn't mad about it. I put on my nightgown wrapped my hair and crawled back in the bed. I turned on the TV and surfed the channels trying to zone out until I fell asleep.

The sound of the water running woke me, Reggie was already in the shower. I did a quick rewind of the previous evening and tried to rationalize it and find a way to mentally let it go and enjoy my mini-vacation. Being at the same motel really wasn't that big of a deal.

"Good morning, beautiful," he said when he came out of the shower with a hot mist following him.

"Good morning yourself," I said with a smile, walking into the bathroom.

I put on a shower cap and climbed into the tub and turned on the shower. I let the hot water relax me. I knew how it felt to be rejected without having the time to show I was worthy. Reggie was a nice guy and I wanted to give us a chance and not get hung up on the small stuff. I stepped out of the shower with the hope of a brand new day. That's when I saw it. He had used both of the frigging towels.

"Excuse you," I yelled out into the room, "What kind of selfish asshole would use both of the towels in here."

"They were so small I needed to use two," he said as if he didn't see the error of his ways.

"Did you not for a minute think that maybe one was for you and one was for me?"

"I'm sorry, I wasn't thinking, usually I'm in a room by myself."

"Are you telling me that you forgot I was out here?" I asked with my aggravation growing.

"Look don't trip, hold up, I'll go and get you some towels front the front desk," he said, throwing on his shirt and shoes and rushing out the door.

This is unbelievable, as hard as I try to keep the door open for this man he keeps making me want to slam it. I was standing in the floor butt naked and dripping dry, this was so so wrong. I grabbed a hand towel and went over to the bed in an attempt to dry myself off.

"What are you doing?" Reggie asked when he came back in the room.

"What does it look like? I'm air drying and using a hand towel because of the inconsideration of someone else."

"I know you didn't try to dry your ass with that little towel," he said laughing, "You know you are lucky it didn't get lost."

"You got jokes?" I said, unable to feel the humor, "You are cracking yourself up."

"If you used it to dry under your breast it would have disappeared there too," he laughed, continuing his impromptu performance.

"Enough with the jokes, Reggie, give me a towel. I thought you wanted to make up for the mess you did the last time we hooked up."

"You're right, I'm sorry. I really like you, but it seems like I can't do anything right when I'm with you."

"That goes without saying," I said, grabbing my travel bag and going into the bathroom.

Now what? How can I talk myself into looking over this last episode? I wasn't ready to hurry back home and if I read him too hard he might not drive me back. Those were reasons enough for me to get dressed, comb my hair, put my make-up on, complete with a smile, and have a good time.

I gave myself a word of advice before I walked out, "Keep your expectations low."

"What's for breakfast, big money?" I asked, making a joke of my own.

"Funny, we're going to your favorite place, Mickey D's," he said, waiting for a response.

"Let's go, I have a taste for a McGriddle and some orange juice," I said, walking out the door in front of him.

Reggie followed me out. Walking to the car I could feel his eyes watching me. I had him where I wanted him, confused. I know he expected me to give him another earful but I wasn't going there. I intended to have the fantastic day I deserved no matter what.

"What do you feel like doing?" he asked after we had breakfast.

"Why don't we go and walk in the mall and then go see a movie."

I was in my own private heaven for a few hours. We walked through the mall hand-in-hand window shopping with him telling me all the things he wanted to buy for me when he got his money straight. Then later in the movies we sat with his arm around the back of my seat and I leaned my head on his shoulder. It was truly romantic; I didn't even mind that he didn't buy us any of the snacks. It was all about being together, a couple.

After the movie we bought some fried chicken and went back to the room. We ate and talked and then we watched TV for a while. When we had sex that night I have to admit that it was better than the other times and he made sure we had extra towels.

"Let's get an early start and I'll make you breakfast when we get to my house." I suggested in the morning.

"I wish I could take you home with me instead of Pulaski," he told me when we put out bags in the trunk."

"That might be nice, get me a job in Atlanta and I'll be on the midnight train to Georgia."

"I'm going to hold you to that," he said, starting the car.

"Do that."

We grooved to the music on the radio while I watched the exits quickly roll and countdown to mine. It hadn't been a bad couple of days; I had scratched my itch and enjoyed his company in spite of a few hiccups. Reggie got my bag out of the trunk while I unlocked the front door. I could hear the TV playing in the living room.

"Mama," I yelled out to let her know it was me before I walked in the room, "I'm back."

She turned around with a disgusted look on her face and asked, "Who's this?"

"This is my friend Reggie, he took me up to Nashville for a few days," I said, feeling embarrassed that she didn't remember him.

"Umph," was the only comment she had before she turned back towards the television.

"I'm going to get back on the road," Reggie said, grabbing my hand, "Don't worry about cooking breakfast."

"This is what time it is," I said as I walked him to the door.

"Stay strong, that's all we can do," he said as he leaned down and gave me a soft kiss on the cheek.

"I don't have a choice," I replied, mentally subtracting some of his points from the bad column and added them to the good one.

"Mama, do you need anything, I'm going to make myself something to eat?" I asked, going into the kitchen.

"Yeah, baby, Thomas didn't give me anything to eat this morning," she shouted behind me.

Inside the kitchen sink I could see the breakfast dishes laying there where Thomas had dumped them; it was as good as his signature. He had been by this morning and she had forgotten. I'm sure my daddy was in the bed sleeping, I had seen his car in the driveway. I scrambled some eggs and made some toast for both of us, I did not feel like arguing with her over whether she had breakfast or not. I took her a plate and sat down with mine in the kitchen to go through the mail.

Among the junk mail and the usual bills was a letter addressed to me, not one I had prayed for but the one I had dreaded. It was from my student loan servicing center. It was time to pay the piper. I laughed to myself but I could have cried. The irony was when I borrowed the money I was positive that my education was going to pay off. I was going to get a good paying job and live my life. Paying the money back was never a worry. Now I'm broke with just a piece of a job and I can't afford the payments. I toyed with the idea of calling them for a deferment but I decided to wait, something had to give sooner or later.

***

"I'm so glad this is our last class," DeQuan, the rude boy of the semester, blurted out when he came into the classroom.

"Yes, it is the last day of class," I said, feeling mixed emotions about it. "I'm going to need you all to fill out a survey about this class before the final exam. Once you are done with the survey I'll give you the test and when you are finished you may hand it in and you are dismissed. Jayla would you give me a hand handing these out to the class?" I asked, handing her the stack of surveys.

"No problem, Dr. King, I got you," she said, smacking her gum.

I looked through the messages on my phone while the class colored in the small circles that gave their opinion of me as a teacher. I thought I had done a good job with what I had to work with, most of them had passed the class. One by one they turned in the survey, took the exam, and handed in their papers before they left. I smiled at some of the whoops and celebratory howls in the hallway as they walked away. It may have been torture for some of them but it had been my life preserver, I was going under before this opportunity lifted my spirits.

"That's that," I said to Dr. Glover, the Biology Department coordinator, when I turned in my manila envelope of surveys on my way out.

"Good job, Dr. King," he said with a smile, "This class isn't taught in the summer and we don't have any others open. We'll contact you in the next few weeks if we're going to need you for the fall semester.

"Thank you, sir, I look forward to hearing from you," I told him as I walked out of the office. "Damn," I hissed when I was sure I was out of earshot, "I was out of a job again."

The summer months were hot as hell but my Mama and me were hibernating like two grizzly bears with attitudes. The University of Phoenix was playing me off and my only connection to the outside world beside my mandatory visits to Wal-Mart was my cell phone. For the most part I just listened to voicemails and read texts messages, I didn't want anybody to know I was unemployed and all non-void. I was still job hunting and submitting applications on-line but my morale was way down. I had gone from being a major contender in the game to being an underdog. There were days that the the only reason I got up in the morning was to keep them from hitting me while I'm down.

I needed a new strategy I thought, a supernatural intervention. I needed a fresh blessing. "Maybe the Lord can't hear my prayers from bedside Baptist, so I'm going to church," I said to my reflection in the mirror after rising up early on Sunday morning. It may be a long-shot; I don't know if any of these preachers have any connection to the Almighty with all the womanizing, down-low activities, criminal charges, and law suits in the mix. It seems like that's where the devil goes to recruit for his army.

I took a hot bath, lotioned up and down, sprayed on some cologne, and then searched in the closet for one of my bright colorful sundresses to wear and some strappy sandals. I remembered Pastor Andrew's words the last time I was in church, even though I won't mention how long that has been, "Sometimes you have to fake it until you make it." Just because I didn't feel that great at the moment didn't mean I had to look like it. I stood in the mirror putting on some lavender colored eye shadow and I could feel the change coming over me and I hadn't even got to a pew yet.

"Hallelujah," I shouted to the ceiling after I found a boiled egg in the refrigerator, "This with a bowl of instant oatmeal and buttered toast and Mama is good."

I finished her breakfast in no time and was headed to the house of the Lord humming with the gospel choir singing on the radio.

At the time for altar call, I sashayed down front. I asked for a special prayer for my mama's health and healing and for a door of opportunity to open for me somewhere in the name of Jesus. I listened intently and the message was about being "pregnant with possibilities." I wasn't sure if I was, but if I claimed it, nobody could deny it.

Before the service was over my belly was growling like the bear I had pretended to be. In all my excitement I had not eaten a bite. I held my stomach in tight to minimize the grumbling,

I didn't want to bring any extra attention to myself. After the message I bowed my head and eased out during the invitation. I didn't have any money for offering and I didn't want to be one of those who sat in their seat when everybody else went to the altar.

I was so hungry I stopped at the Wal-Mart to get a couple pieces of chicken even though I hated to swipe my card for less than $5 dollars. I stood impatiently in the line and that's when I saw the sign that they were hiring. I paid for my chicken and pulled out a leg to chew on as soon as I got in my car to appease my empty belly. It definitely wasn't the job I wanted but it would serve the purpose at that moment. That's when I decided to put in an application at Wal-Mart minus the degrees and teaching experience; I needed to make some money. Being proud and empty-handed are a mismatched couple that should be separated.

***

"I hope this is good news," Jazz said when she answered the phone, "I haven't heard from you in months."

"It's not bad news," I said, ignoring the rest of her comment, "I'm getting a new attitude."

"That is good news," she said laughing.

"You are not going to worry me today; I just called to catch up on what's going on around there."

"Your main squeeze, Curtis, graduated and so did Anika," she said, waiting for my reaction.

"I hate that I missed his defense and another chance to wrap him up but I'm not ready to see anybody until I get on my feet."

"So what's been keeping you so busy you can't return a call?"

"Not much, I was in town after the holidays."

"You didn't call," she said with an attitude, "Where did you stay?"

"Reggie came and picked me up," I said, taking my turn to wait for a reaction.

"For real?" she asked. "I thought you had closed that book."

"I did, but I had to pick it back up. I was lonely and feeling unwanted. My mother was worrying me and I had to get my groove back."

"Wow, so how did that work out?"

"He was damn near as broke as I was, but it wasn't bad."

"You know I'm old school, the Isley Brothers said, *Love the one you're with*."

"It held me for a minute and now I'm hungry again. That's why I told you I don't like long distance relationships."

"That is not a relationship, both of you are making booty calls, but I'm not mad at you. Anyway how's your mom doing?"

"Basically, she's the same. I really called to tell you that I got a part-time job."

"Now you're talking, are you back teaching again?"

"No, I haven't heard back from them. I'm working at Wal-Mart."

"Stop playing, Tia," she said, waiting for the punch line.

"I'm not playing, I saw they were hiring, I put in an application, they called me for an interview, and I got a job."

"Girl, you have been making some crazy moves but

173

sometime you got to do what you got to do. It will keep some change in your pocket until you get something better."

"My sentiments exactly, so I called to let you know I'm all right."

"I'm glad you did, finally, and since you got a j. o. b. I want to see you for homecoming."

"I may do that, I'll let you know," I said before I hung up.

I put on my work shirt and badge after I got Mama's lunch made and headed off for my five-hour shift. Walking inside the building I couldn't help but think this wasn't the door I had in mind when I sent up my prayer but I was grateful for anything. If this was my lesson in humility, I want to say it has been well taught and learned; I have made honors and would like to move on to the next lesson and put this one behind me.

One evening after two months of aching legs and feet from standing on concrete I got a phone call from Marissa Phillips, a former fellow student who was working at the University of Georgia. I was so tired I accidently answered before I screened the call; I still was out of touch with most people.

"How are things going, Tia?" she asked kindly. "I've been thinking about you and it took more than a minute to find somebody who had your number."

"I'm hanging in there, Marissa" I said, surprised to hear from her after three years, "I heard you went to Atlanta, how have you been?"

"I'm good, I can't complain. I'm submitting my own grant and I have a post-doc position within it that I need someone to commit to and you came to mind."

"Seriously?" I asked, feeling like I was on the edge of my blessing.

"Yeah, I heard about a year ago that you were still looking for a position. Did you find one that you're happy with?"

"Nothing that I'm happy with yet," I answered, ashamed to mention that I was a member of the Wal-Mart family.

"Would you consider moving to Atlanta and working with me in my lab?"

"Yes, I definitely would," I said, hiding the height of my enthusiasm."

"Fantastic. I need your e-mail, I'm going to add your name to the grant and I need to have a copy of your CV and some other information that has to be submitted."

"Not a problem, I can get it all to you by the end of the day," I said eagerly.

"That sounds good, Tia, this is great, but I want to caution you that everything is contingent upon my receiving the grant."

"I understand, and I truly want to thank you for thinking about me, I really appreciate it."

"I know your work ethic and the kind of research you're capable of. You would be helping me out and I want to do the same for you."

"Thanks again for calling, Marissa," I said before I hung up and thanked God that I had answered the phone.

I sat down to rub my feet, to absorb the phone call, and to think about Marissa. She had done something so exceptional for me even though we had never been close friends. I had not invested much in the social relationships with other female students while I was in school. Most of my focus had been on the men and trying to find my husband and now the most valuable person to me at this moment was someone I had barely given the time of day. I promised myself that from this point that I would be more cognizant and caring of the people I come in contact with, female and male.

11

Chapter Eleven

"**M**ama, I've got some good news," I said, walking into the living room, "Somebody that I went to grad school with at TSU just called me about a job."

"That's how it goes," she said, keeping her eyes on the TV, "As soon as you get a job then another one comes."

"Yeah, Mama, that's how it goes."

I thought about saying more, challenging the TV for her attention to let her know how much this meant to me but I knew it would only frustrate me more. My mother was there in the room but I had lost my confidant, my oldest friend, my head cheerleader, and my biggest critic. The prospect made me feel like she was abandoning me. Intellectually, I knew it was totally against her will but to me it didn't seem like she wasn't even trying to hold on to her mental state.

"I'm going to fix some dinner," I said, leaving the room.

"All right, baby, I sure am hungry."

The ground beef had browned but the water for the pasta had not yet boiled when my phone vibrated on the counter. I had to smile when I saw it was Reggie.

"Are you here yet?" I asked, teasing him.

"You see how you do me, if you call me I'll be there."

"Don't say things you don't mean."

"How's the job hunt going?" he asked, changing the subject.

I wasn't ready to talk about it yet so I said, "Not much different."

"Do you wanna work for me?" he asked in his Big Willy voice.

"How much does it pay?" I asked jokingly.

"Don't you wanna know what it is?"

"It doesn't matter right now, I need to get paid."

"I'm seriously looking to hire you."

"I hear you, go on and tell me what you're taking applications for."

"I want you to be my sex slave," he said, trying to sound sexy.

"Is this full-time or by the hour?" I asked, going along with his game.

"I'm going to pay your mileage, everything, by the hour, I'm serious, let's negotiate."

"Not only have you gone crazy the fact is you can't afford me."

"That's cold, Tia. By the way, how is your car holding up?"

"Why, are you going to buy me a new one?"

"It depends on what I get in return."

"You have a lot of leeway if we're talking about a new vehicle."

"I feel like I need some ABC or some XYZ."

"So you're saying if I do XYZ you're going to buy me a car.

"Yes ma'am, baby, I can afford it."

"Are we talking about a 2013?"

"A 2013, no, a 2011, yes, just tell me when you want it."

"Whenever, baby, pull it in the driveway and it's on."

"Don't be surprised," he said as if he had a secret.

"That's the least of my worries," I said, laughing, "If you make me burn this sauce, my mama is going to raise holy hell."

"I'll call you back later, I want you to meet me in Nashville next week."

"Okay, cool" I said, hanging up. I was making some change for the gas and I wanted to celebrate the possibility that I might finally have a job.

Dinner was tasty if I do so say myself. I cleaned the kitchen, and got Mama settled in her room before I ran a hot bubble bath for a treat. I relaxed for a while and then I called Jazz, it was definitely time for an update.

"Hey, what are you up to?" I asked after she said hello.

"I'm tired of trying to find something on the television."

"I am soaking in a well deserved hot tub of water."

"You deserve it, girl, enjoy."

"I had to call you, I talked to Reggie earlier today and my boo-thang is going to buy me a car."

"Oh really, is he the latest lotto winner or something?"

"I don't know, maybe he got a big commission check or a bonus."

"He's so out the box, I wouldn't believe it until I see it."

"I'm not, but I got a call from Marissa, you remember her, she graduated a couple of years before me, she's at the University of Georgia. She offered me a position in her lab if she gets her grant funded."

"That's the best news I've heard in a long time, I'm happy for you and her. I'll have to pray that it comes through."

"It's got to, I can't make it much longer working at Wally's world."

"How long before she gets the decision?"

"She said that they have ninety days to review it."

"That means you should be ready to start out the New Year with your goals back on track."

"I hope so, Jazz, I don't want to waste anymore time."
"The time isn't wasted, Tia, it has served a purpose. You may have needed some down time to get your mind refreshed again."

"It is so encouraging to know that you still have on those rose-colored glasses."

"Why would I take them off when the view looks so good?"

"I've got to go, my water is getting cold" I said, not wanting to get emotional on the phone."

"All right, girl, keep in touch," she said.

The waiting wasn't easy so I planned a weekend in Nashville to take my mind off of it. It would also let my daddy and Thomas know that they couldn't always rely on me to take care of Mama. I had a life of my own too. Reggie said he would be there for the weekend and I was jonesing for some loving. This wasn't the relationship I wanted but if I got the job in Atlanta we would get the chance to see if it could work.

The night before we planned to meet I got a text from Reggie that said, "It's my weekend to have the kids but I still want to see you. I'll work something out. Can't wait until tomorrow."

I packed my weekend bag the night before and took it with me on my shift. I always felt guilty whenever I left Mama, so one goodbye for the day was enough for me. I changed clothes in the employee's restroom at work and got on the road around 6:00. I sent Reggie a text that I was on my way.

He texted me back, "Meet me at the Qdoba Restaurant on West End when you get here."

This rendezvous was getting off to a good start. I pumped up the radio and pressed a little harder on the gas. It was hard to believe that it had been six long months since the last time we'd been together. I got to the Mexican restaurant in record time. I saw his car in the parking lot when I pulled up. I ran a comb through my hair, put on some fresh lip gloss and went inside.

"Mmm, you look good," he said, standing up and giving me a hug.

"It's good to see you," I said, looking at him like he was an extra-large burrito and I had not eaten in days.

He sat down and looked at his hands while he talked, "I had to bring my children here with me."

"Okay, I want to meet them anyway, we can make some adjustments. It will be fun."

"There's another problem," he said, still avoiding eye contact.

"What's that?" I asked, waiting for the second bomb to drop.

"It's my ex, she came with us," he said in a low voice.

"What in the hell are you talking about?" I asked, totally confused.

"When I told her I was taking them out of town she said she was going too. Then the kids got happy about it and there was nothing I could do. They're all at the hotel room."

"This is bullshit, Reggie, it doesn't make any sense. Who takes their ex on a road trip with their kids to go see another woman? Did you forget to tell her that you were going to see me? Does she even know about me?"

"I don't know why she wanted to come, what was I supposed to do? She thought the kids would be alone when I had to work."

"First of all who works on Friday and Saturday on campus looking for a salesman? You were supposed to tell her that you had plans to spend the weekend with a female friend. Why didn't you call and tell me this when I told you I was on my way? I would not have even come."

"If you can get a room we can still have some time together."

"Negro, you have a lot of nerve. Do you actually think you are going to sneak over and screw me for fifteen minutes and then sneak back in the room with you family. That's not going to happen, you've got me mixed up."

I practically knocked over the table getting out of there. I couldn't believe he had played me like that. I stomped over to my car and slammed the door after I got in. I didn't even have enough money to pay for a hotel because I hadn't planned on staying in a motel by myself. I wanted to cry but I was so damn pissed off I couldn't. I wasn't in any shape to drive back. Where could I stay? I got out my cell phone and called Wayne.

"I'm in town and I need somewhere to stay," I said, sounding distressed, "Can I come over?"

"Tia, what's wrong, what's going on? You know you are always welcome to stay with me at any time," he answered sincerely.

"Nothing's wrong, I came up for some plans in town that changed and I don't feel like driving back tonight."

"Come on by, girl, I want to see you."

"I'll be there in twenty minutes," I said, relieved that he was home and I had somewhere to lay my head for the night.

The apartment complex was so familiar, this was one place where time had stood still, at least outside in the parking lot. I had a lot of memories during the time I spent here with Wayne, we'd had our share of fun, probably because I never took our relationship seriously. I knocked on the door thankful that we had always remained friends.

"What the hell?" I said, jumping back from the shock.

Wayne had answered the door butt naked. He used to do some crazy things back in the day but this was over the top. This whole day was insane. I looked around in the bushes for a camera because I know I'm being punked right now, there's no doubt about it.

"Don't play with me I'm not in the mood, Wayne," I said, keeping my eyes down on the ground, "You need to put some clothes on your ass."

"Come on, Tia, I know you have five minutes for me," he said, standing there like he was a rational human being.

I pushed by him dragging my bag, afraid that somebody had already witnessed this insanity. He closed the door and we stood in the floor looking at each other for a minute.

"What is this about?" I asked finally, "We haven't got down like that in three years."

"I missed you," he said, walking towards me.

"I can't say another word to you until you get dressed, for real."

Wayne walked out and I flopped down on the couch in the

living room. I needed somebody to play Mary J.'s 'No more Drama' on full blast. Wayne came back in the room with gym shorts and a t-shirt and I threw up a quick praise to the Lord.

"I thought when you called you were ready to come home to Daddy," he said, sitting beside me on the couch.

"No, that wasn't it, I was supposed to meet somebody here for the weekend and I got stood up. It blew me away and I couldn't make the drive back home tonight so I called you."

"You know that I'm always here for you," he said, reaching down and taking off my shoes and starting to rub my feet.

"We are just friends, Wayne, and that's the way I like it."

"Are you saying you don't ever think about how good we were when we were together?" he asked while he massaged my toes.

"You and I must remember two different things, I was always keeping your kids and you were always running around on me."

"That was young man stuff, I'm past all that now."

"Wayne, you were in your late thirties, that's not a young man to me, you're not going to do right at whatever age."

"I will for you," he said, smiling.

"Just be my friend, that's what I need more than a man right now," I practically pleaded with him. "Dig something out of that refrigerator to feed me and then give me a blanket so I can go to sleep. Would you do that for me?"

"Whatever you want, baby," he said, laying my feet on the couch and walking to the kitchen, "I got you."

I laid my head back on the couch looking at the ceiling for ten minutes before I finally relaxed and closed my eyes. What's wrong with me I asked myself? Why do I keep getting caught in these messed up situations?

This relationship with Reggie was starting to stink like one I had with this guy name Kevin. I met him when I was working weekends at Walgreens after I started grad school at TSU. He was about six-feet-tall, medium brown like a walnut shell with his hair cut short in a fade. He wasn't the type I usually went for; he was a slim built pretty boy who liked to dress.

He started giving me a ride home when I got off work and soon he was dropping me off too. We went to church every Sunday and would go out to eat during the week. I had even taken him home and introduced him to Mama and Daddy.

"That boy you brought here before looks gay to me," Daddy said over the dinner table the next time I came home for a visit.

"He is not gay, Daddy, why are you saying that?" I said, scrunching up my face to keep from choking on my food.

"He is sweet as sugar," Mama chimed in, "How many straight guys do you know that have a ring on their tongue."

"Case closed," Daddy said before he bit into his chicken breast.

"I don't believe y'all," I said exasperated, "Neither one of you have anything good to say about anybody I bring home."

"Then you need to bring home some better selections," Mama said, laughing.

"It's my choice, and I choose who I like, you don't have to like him," I protested.

"You've got that right," Mama said, getting seconds on the mashed potatoes.

Kevin was cool with me, he was a gentleman but he made my

bed rock when we got busy. I thought it was all good until this girl named Natalie came up to the register one day when I was in the pharmacy.

This chick comes in with an over-due-for-a-touch-up blonde weave and painted on denim capris and asks, "Can you tell me what I need to take for sinus headaches and allergies?"

"Yes, at the end of the next aisle over there, there is a section that has several things you can try," I said, pointing her in the direction.

She kept standing there so I asked her, "Is there something else you need?"

"I'm in here to tell you that Kevin has been seeing us both at the same time," she said, putting her hand on her hip, "I found out that he hangs with me while you're at work or at school."

I was stunned. I didn't need this ghetto mess. I was trying to get through my day and get home to hit the books. I had an exam the next day and I don't play with my grades.

"I'm sorry to hear that, but if that's what he's been doing, then I'm done, you can have him," I told her, hoping she would leave before another customer came behind her.

"My name is Natalie, and I'm a crazy bitch and we need to go and confront him. Once I came in here and talked to you I could see that you are a nice person and I decided to let you know what's going on."

"Thanks for letting me know, Natalie, but it's not that deep for me. We weren't boyfriend and girlfriend so you can do whatever you want because I'm through with him."

"Okay, sister," she said, hitting the counter and nodding her head before she turned on her high heels, "I'm going to show him that players don't always win."

After she left I told my boss I felt sick and needed to leave early, I didn't want to be there when Kevin came to pick me up. There was nothing left to say.

***

I must have dozed off on the sofa because when I woke up Wayne was rubbing me on the thigh with one hand and holding a bacon sandwich in the other saying, "I thought you wanted something to eat?"

"I do," I said, sitting up and sliding my feet back on the floor, "You are a lifesaver."

"So what's up with the nigga who stood you up?" he asked, sitting beside me.

"I don't even know what to tell you," I said, crunching on the crispy bacon.

"Was he supposed to be your man?"

"Not really, we were trying to get to know each other, but it's really too complicated for me to deal with. I don't know what the hell is going on."

"I don't know why you won't move in with me and let me take care of you," he said, rubbing on my thigh again.

"Wayne, we've been through that, I need a man with a real job and some benefits to take care of me, we can't live on the money you make bootlegging CDs."

"I've got my own place, Tia. I pay my bills, and you see I can feed you. I love you, what more do you need?"

"I don't know, Wayne," I said, shaking my head. "Put in one of those comedy DVD's you're hustling so I can get a laugh.

We watched movies until we fell asleep. In the morning after I showered I still wasn't ready to go back home. I needed more

187

of a break from home but I didn't feel like listening to Wayne profess his love all day. Hopefully I could crash at Jason's or Denise's tonight. I called Jazz to see if she wanted to hang out.

"Where are you, are you in Nashville?" she asked, surprised to hear from me so early.

"Yeah, I'm in town, I came up for the weekend but my plans went crazy."

"What happened?"

"It's a long story; I don't even want to talk about it on the phone."

"Well, I'll treat you to lunch after you pour your guts out," she said with a laugh, "Where do you want to go?"

"You know me and Red Lobster."

"Yes, you're stuck on it and you need to let it go. Come on by the house when you get yourself together and I'll drive, I need to put some clothes in the cleaners on the way."

I drove by the campus after I left Wayne's apartment. I don't know why, maybe to see if things had changed any since I graduated. I looked at the students walking around and I envied them. When you're a student it gives you that feeling of being young, like time is standing still. Since I've been out it feels like time is rushing by so fast despite the fact my life is stuck on pause. If Marissa hadn't called me about a post-doc position I wouldn't even have any hope of getting to press the start button.

I got over to Jasmine's house around 11:30. She was outside talking to her hubby while he was working in the yard. That's the picture I want for myself. I hear some women say that don't need a man, they're fine by themselves, but I want to share my life with somebody.

"Hey, Tia," Jasmine yelled when she saw me drive by the mailbox in front on the house, "Park on the street and I'll pull out the car."

"Did y'all have any plans for today?" I asked, getting in the car, I didn't want to cause a problem in their happy home.

"Not at all, I'm sure he's glad I'm getting out of the house. Now he can work all day in the yard in peace. My question to you is why can't you keep the scissors out of your hair?" she asked after she saw I was sporting a mini small afro. "Women are out here buying hair by the pound spending small fortunes and you've got a beautiful head of hair but you want to be bald. I simply can't understand that."

"I cut the perm out; I think I want to go natural."

"Don't get me wrong, Tia," Jazz said, hopping on the interstate towards Rivergate, "I'm down with natural but not everybody appreciates our naturalness. Do you think you should have played it safe and stuck with the flat-iron and the make-up until we get you a job and a man?"

"I'm not about to change myself for anybody, they have to accept me as I am."

"I hear you, I'm on Team Tia, but I always have to give you the other side to think about," she said, turning down the radio. "Anyway, let's get back to what you are doing in the big city?"

"I came to hook-up with Reggie again."

"I'm going to give you a pass on that one, girl, because I know that the flesh has a mind of its own. So what drama did he perform this time?"

"This one is award winning, this Negro came to Nashville to see me with his kids and his wife with him in the car. He acted real shady meeting me in the restaurant while they waited at the motel. I feel like I don't know whether to believe him or not. He's always tried to keep me under cover and out of sight."

"See, now you are going to make me pull this car over before I have a wreck. I can't even believe anybody would be that bold."

"He said that it was his weekend to have the kids, so he didn't have any choice but to bring them, but then she decided that if he was taking them out of town she was going too."

"Why didn't he just tell her that he wasn't going on a camping trip? All he really had to do was tell her that he was going to get his itch scratched."

"I don't know what to think, it's so over the top," I said as Jasmine pulled in a parking space at Red Lobster.

"I don't want to be the bearer of bad news and you know I always try to see the good in any situation but I'm starting to think Reggie is not as separated as he says. I mean they rode up here like one big happy family for a fun-filled weekend. You're the only one who didn't fit in the picture."

"I know he didn't think he was going to do the family thing all day and then sneak in my room for a quickie after they went to sleep. Why would he even call me for that?"

"He had it all figured out until Wifey said she was coming at the last minute."

A hostess showed us to a table and I thought about all the ways I would beat Reggie's ass if I could be alone with him for twenty minutes. If he had played me like that I would definitely have to take him down. I was sure Jazz could see the steam coming out of the top of my head.

"Go on and order what you want, Tia, it's my treat. Given that you don't drink, you are definitely going to have to eat."

"As long as you know what time it is, Jazz," I said, opening up the menu.

I ordered enough food for two people. I ate all of it and enjoyed every bite. I even ordered some dessert to take with me.

"By the way, where did you stay last night?" Jazz asked.

"I called Wayne and asked him could I come over. He was tripping at first, thinking I was going to give him a flashback."

"You might need to think twice about Wayne. He's crazy about you and he is really nice to you. We might need to re-evaluate your analysis of the situation, especially if he can rock that world. Who says you need a man with a high IQ, then you'll have another problem with him trying to run your life."

"How many times have I told you that I'm not going to settle? I know what I want and I'll just have to wait until I find it."

"All right, I'll give you two more years of that talk, and then if you're still single we will re-visit this conversation. Let's go walk some of these calories we've eaten off shopping in the mall," Jazz said on the way to the car.

"Not today," I said, thinking that the realization that Reggie has been playing me has me too upset to shop, "My money is still funny and they don't have a lot of selection in there for big girls. I think I'll just drive on back home. My mood is really messed up."

"I know you have trust issues and it really bothers you when a guy lies to you, but remember you're not in love with him or anything. He wasn't the man of your dreams so don't get messed up about it."

"I'm not," I told her, "It's just that I've got a lot to deal with right now and I don't need the extra bullshit."

"I think it's time to play your theme song again," Jazz said, "When's the last time you heard it? You're letting folks get to you."

That's when I felt my phone vibrate and it was a text from my brother, Thomas. I was so glad Jazz was driving instead of me when I read it, "I just asked Sharron if she wanted to get married and she said yes."

12

Chapter Twelve

It was a long ride back to Pulaski. I hate that feeling when it seems like everybody has something positive going on in their lives but you. When I opened the door of the house my mama was in her favorite position, parked in front of the television.

"Hey, Mama," I said giving a hug around her shoulders before I sat down in the chair on the left side of her. "Have you been doing okay?" I asked, trying to get her attention.

"I'm doing fine, Tia," she answered without looking at me.

This was getting harder to take because as time passed she didn't seem interested in me or any part of my life. She had always been here for me to talk to and now she couldn't care less what was going on with me. I know she's sick and it's not intentional but I need her and it doesn't even seem like she's trying to hold on or connect with anybody outside of TV land. Things have been like this for a while but I still missed her nosiness, the judgments, and the off-handed remarks about my friends and the guys I dealt with.

"Mama, Thomas texted me that he and Sharron are getting married, did he tell you?" I asked.

"I don't know what that boy is doing, he don't need to marry anybody. He got enough on his hands with all his kids. Can you get me something to drink, baby, I'm so thirsty?"

"Sure, Mama," I said, taking off my jacket and leaving it on the chair before I got up and went into the kitchen. I handed her the glass of sweet tea. "Where's Daddy?"

"I don't know, maybe he's at work," she said nonchalantly.

"How long have you been here by yourself?"

"Tia, I keep telling you I'm a grown woman, I don't need nobody to babysit me."

Not in the mood to be put in my place yet again I went in the kitchen to make some dinner. It was perfect timing when my daddy finally showed up. I had just finished the spaghetti and coleslaw for the catfish I had fried.

"Hey, Tia, I didn't expect to see you back home today," he said, giving me a kiss on the back of my head.

"Me either, Daddy," I said, "How long have you been gone? Mama was here by herself when I got home."

"I've got to do what I have to do to keep the roof over our heads, baby girl. Your mama was fine when you got here wasn't she?"

"Yeah, she was, but she could have fallen or tried to cook something and forgot about it."

"You have got to stop worrying about your mama and get yourself together. Time is moving on and you haven't found a job yet."

"Daddy, I've done all I can to make that happen and nothing has broken for me yet."

"I not complaining or trying to put pressure on you, baby, I just want you to focus on your life and not your mama and me."

Washing his hands at the sink, he said, "I got this here, you do what you need to do. Your brother, Thomas, is moving right on, he's asked that girl he's running around with to get married."

"So I've heard. All I know is, if they have a wedding ceremony I'm not going to be in it."

"It's his second time around so he doesn't need to make a big fuss about it. Oh yeah, there was a letter for you in the mail today," he said, passing by me with two plates of food, one for him and one for Mama.

I rushed over to the basket on the kitchen counter where we placed the mail and I could see the University of Georgia letter head sticking out behind the electric bill. I snatched it up and hurried back to my bedroom to get the verdict. I didn't want anybody to see me if it was more bad news. I didn't know how I was going to react.

Thank God, it was encouraging news. Marissa had gotten a good review on her grant and she felt like she should get her approval letter before Thanksgiving. I picked up my cell and pressed her name.

"Hello, Marissa, I got the good news," I said excitedly into the phone after she answered.

"I am so happy," she said, "Soon I'll be able to set up my own lab. Once I get the final approval it will probably take another month to get the paperwork set up and then I'll offer you a contract. I think you should start making plans to get here by the first of the year."

"That sounds like a plan and I really want to thank you for thinking of me and giving me this opportunity, it means more to me than you know."

"I know how hard it is to find that first job and get started. Somebody took a chance and gave me a break so I want to do the same for someone else. Besides, I know that you can handle your business in the lab."

"I can hardly wait," I told her, "We'll be the dynamic duo, you'll be Batman and I'll be Robin."

"I love it, Tia, now I can laugh again with some of the pressure off."

"You and me both."

"I'll keep in touch."

"Thanks again, Dr. Phillips."

"Bye, Dr. King."

***

Six weeks later Marissa's grant was awarded and I had received the job offer. It wasn't big money but it was employment and it would take care of me and my bills. I couldn't wait to give my two-week notice at Wal-Mart. Things were finally turning around for me and I could not have been more relieved. I was even happy for Thomas when he had his semi-ghetto Christmas wedding and reception at the community center. Not only that, I even kept my mouth shut when I saw that the ham between the biscuits his new wife Sharron had served was slightly green.

I didn't think anything could spoil my mood until I heard Sharron announce that she and Thomas were moving to Murfreesboro. It was a cold day in December but I broke out in a sweat and my smile melted and rolled down my face into a frown. I scanned the gym of the center, looking for the groom. Through the crowd of guests I caught a glimpse of my daddy talking while he stood behind Mama in her wheel chair. She sat there looking at our folks like they were strangers. When I spotted Thomas laughing with some of his homies I was on full speed ahead.

"Thomas, what's up?" I said, pushing past his friends like they weren't there, "You didn't say anything about moving out of town."

"Yeah, Sharron's job is there and they're hiring too, so we gotta do what we gotta do."

"What about Mama?" I asked, exasperated. He didn't do anything but think about himself.

"What about her?" he asked as if he was confused and had a taste of Alzheimers too.

"Daddy needs help to look after her when he's at work. You know I'm getting ready to move to Atlanta in a few weeks for a job. I was hoping that you could look after Mama and give me a chance to get on my feet."

"I got my own family to worry about. I love my mama but I got to do what's best for them first."

"Thomas, you never really helped that much when I was here anyway but I need you to pinch in more now so I can go and get my career started. I've been at home for over two years. I can't turn this down; it's the only chance I've gotten."

"Nobody is telling you to turn it down. We can deal with this later. In case you forgot, this is my wedding day," he said, walking away to get a beer out of the cooler.

He always got the last jab even when we were younger. I stood there trying to come up with my plan B. Then I decided that if push came to shove I would have to take Mama with me to Atlanta. I couldn't lose this chance, I've been out of school for three years and I'm closer to forty years old than I am to thirty.

"Tia," my daddy called from the other side of the room. I crossed through the center court of the floor to get to him. "Your mama is getting tired," he said. "You mind helping me get her on home?"

"No, Daddy, I'm ready to leave anyway."

We got Mama settled in bed despite her protests to let her stay up and watch some television. We were all exhausted so we needed to get her situated while we were still moving around. My daddy got a beer out of the refrigerator and sat down at the kitchen table.

"What's on your mind, Tia? You were on cloud nine when we left this afternoon, now you look like you're scraping the ground. You not having them somebody-else's-wedding-day blues again are you?"

"Not this time, Daddy, but I am worried about not being able to go to Atlanta in a few weeks for my job."

"What do you mean, have they changed their minds?"

"No, Daddy, with your job hours and Thomas moving to Murfreesboro you are going to need me to stay around and help you with Mama," I said, barely able to hold my tears of disappointment back behind my eyes.

"Tia, what you don't understand is that your mama is my wife and my responsibility not yours. You're going to have to let me handle it. The doctors have explained to me that the time will come when we can't manage your mama's care here at the house without fulltime help. I've accepted that and you're going to have to accept it too."

"Mama is not going to agree to go into any kind of nursing home and you know that."

"Your mama is leaving us a little more everyday and there's nothing we can do about it. It's not what we want but that's the reality."

"Maybe I shouldn't leave right now, I can keep looking for something close to home."

"The only thing that you need to concern yourself with is getting to Atlanta so you can start using that piece of paper it took you so long to get."

"I've been waiting for so long and now I'm not ready. They want me there in less than three weeks and I haven't even thought about where I'm going to live."

"We'll work it out," he assured me. "When the weekend gets here you and I are going to drive down there and find you a place. Thomas and Sharron will have to look after your mama."

"Thanks, Daddy," I said, giving him a hug around his neck before I went to bed.

I slept like a rock knowing that Daddy was going to help me work it out and tomorrow was my last day working at Wal-Mart. It had been hard to deal with, the part-time hours and the petty pay, not to mention the fact that I had a Ph.D. hanging on my wall while I ran around in a blue Wal-Mart shirt every day, but it had helped me pay my car insurance, pay my cell phone bill, and keep a little change in my pocket.

On Saturday morning I packed my weekend bag just in case we spent the night. I called Jasmine before we got on the road to tell her I was on my way to Atlanta.

"Hey, Jazz, you won't believe that Thomas has an attitude

about having to stay at the house while Daddy drives with me to Atlanta."

"Well, that's too bad," she said, chuckling, "He usually gets off free without helping at all, he's long overdue."

"I don't know what we're doing looking for a place though, I don't have enough money for first and last month's rent for an apartment."

"What about Marissa, have you told her your situation?"

"No, she's done so much for me, I don't want to ask her for any more favors."

"I hear you on that. What about Reggie, do you think he would let you stay with him for a while until you get a payday."

"I don't even want to go there, I'm not even sure if he's separated. I talked to him a couple of days ago and he asked me about my job situation, I told him it was still in limbo."

"We're desperate right now, you may have to call him. I don't want you down there homeless and living out of your car."

"I've got to go, my daddy is ready."

"Call me."

"Bye, girl."

It was a crazy trip driving around in Atlanta looking for a place to stay. We started at the campus and worked our way out. It looked like all the apartments near the campus were deep in the hood. Whenever I found an area where I felt safe there was the issue of money, and I didn't have any. An apartment would have to wait until I got a couple of paydays.

"Look here, Tia," Daddy said to me from across the table at a KFC restaurant, "We going to have to come up with another plan. What I'm thinking is we get you set up in one of those

Extended Stay Hotels for a month until you get your first check."

"Daddy, I don't have enough cash to stay in one of those places for a month."

"This is what we're gonna do, I'll borrow some money from the credit union to cover it while we get the down payment for the apartment."

"Are you sure you can do that, Daddy? I don't want to put any extra strain on you."

"That's what I'm gonna do, baby. You've been there for me and your mama when we needed it and I'm going to be here for you."

"Thanks so much, Daddy, I didn't know what I was going to do."

"You're still my baby girl and I'm always here to help you."

I drove back to Nashville with a smile on my face while my daddy laid in the back seat napping. He had shown me that in spite of the criticism that my mama always seem to have for him, he was the man. I thought about how I didn't appreciate how hard he worked and how he never let us down. As far as Mama was concerned he could never do enough but I had to give him his props, he had held us down all these years and was still doing it.

I had the urge to call Reggie when I got back home. I couldn't resist telling him I had gotten a job in town and I had been all around his city.

"I was wondering when you were going to decide to pick up the phone and call me," he said when he answered.

"I haven't seen any missed calls from you or any text messages full of apologies either," I said with my voice full of sarcasm.

"Okay, so it's like that, huh? I knew you were still pissed and were going to be fussing."

"Look, there's a lot going on that you don't know. First, I got a job."

"That's good news, where?"

"In Atlanta, University of Georgia."

"Real talk?"

"Yeah, real talk."

"What kind of shit is that?" he asked, adding some bass in his voice, "You don't have anything to say. You come down here and shit in my woods and you don't even have the gall to call me or text me."

"Come on, Reggie," I said in an effort to bring him back to reality, "We weren't even on speaking terms."

"I guess that's supposed to be my fault."

"If you remember correctly then you'll know that it was."

"I'll take that this time," his said, lowering his tone.

"Anyway, I'll be moving there in a couple of weeks."

"What part of town are you staying?"

"Somewhere temporary for now, unless I can stay with you."

"Tia, I'm going to have to talk to you about that later," he said, suddenly rushing to get off the phone.

I didn't expect him to say anything different, that brother wouldn't know the truth if it walked up and slapped him in the face.

13

Chapter Thirteen

The next two weeks flew by. I packed up a couple of suitcases and loaded up my car to drive to Atlanta. Mama was in her usual place and I don't even know if she understood that I was moving out. Daddy walked me out and gave me a hug and kiss on the cheek after I got the bags in the trunk. He was never one for long goodbyes. Inside the car, I punched in the address on the GPS for the Extended Stay Hotel we reserved on-line and pulled off headed towards the interstate. I turned up the radio to drown out my second thoughts and opened up a Snickers bar to give me strength.

In three and a half hours I was at my destination. Before I could get out of the car I noticed a male and female having a heated discussion in the parking lot. It looked pretty serious so I decided to lay low in my seat until it quieted down. My first instinct was to call 911 but I hadn't been here long enough to know the rules about getting into folks business.

The next thing I know fists are flying and the guy is getting the best shots. It's time to make that call. I reached for my phone about the same moment that I heard the sirens approaching. The guy runs off and this is my chance to grab my suitcases and rush in the front of the hotel. Check-in was quick and I was glad, I had already received my welcome to the hood in the parking lot. I picked up my bags and headed for the elevator to take me to the third floor. I stood there long enough for the female from the scuffle outside to join me.

"I saw what happened out there, are you all right?" I asked, trying not to look at the knot raised up on her forehead while we waited for the doors of the elevator to open.

"Yeah, I'm all right, but he better not bring his ass back here tonight," she said, shaking her injured head with her fists still balled up.

"He probably won't," I said, hoping the words would help calm her down as the doors finally opened. "What floor do you want?" I asked as we stepped into the mirrored box.

"Five," she said with her attitude still in effect.

I pushed in the top circle and then the one marked three. I was relieved that we weren't on the same floor just in case her Floyd Mayweather-wanna-be man came back. Safe inside my room, this would have been the time that I would have called my mama to tell her what happened, except she wasn't interested in anything that didn't come across the TV screen these days. I have to admit I was nervous about going out after the drama so I looked in the phone book for a pizza place that delivered.

The next morning on my way to the University of Georgia campus I felt like I was fourteen years old again going for my first day in high school. Besides that lying ass Reggie, Marissa was the only person I knew in the whole city. Thank God, I remembered how to get to the lab, and even though I had made an effort to get there early, Marissa was already there.

"Welcome, Dr. King, make yourself at home," she said with her arms spread wide. "Choose the bench space where you think you'll be comfortable and I'll show you to your office space. There will be one student rotating in here this semester but for the most part it will be just you and me."

"In that case, I'll take the bench over there by the window if that's all right."

"That's cool with me," she said, leading me out of the lab.

I followed her out into the corridor to the left into my office. I sat my messenger bag with my laptop in it down on the desk. I finally had an office to call my own.

"I know you're familiar with the objectives of the grant so we can go over the preliminary data after you get yourself settled in your space, and let me add again that I'm glad you're here."

"I'm glad to be here, thank you," I added with a smile.

I could tell that Marissa was going to be purely professional and I didn't have a problem with it. She was trying to build her career just like the rest of us. Yet, I must admit that it did feel a bit awkward having our relationship of cohort and friend switch to one of boss and subordinate, but whatever way you sliced it, it was better than my stint at Wal-Mart.

The first month passed by slowly, mainly because my money was tight. I don't know why I didn't lose any weight because I was barely getting one good meal a day. I broke down and called Reggie, I thought he might be good for something, but he texted me back that he was in the process of moving to Nashville for his job. Ain't that a bitch? I deleted his number out of my phone again. I made up my mind that I was done reaching back and trying to make old failed relationships into successes.

When I finally got my first paycheck stub I was ready to shout, now I could move out of the Extended Stay projects. I went directly to the apartments that Daddy and I had settled on when we came apartment hunting, plopped down my deposit, and signed a lease. The first person I called was Jason.

"Hey, friend, it's time to move."

"I'm ready when you are," he said with no questions asked.

Jason's friendship was more valuable than gold and more secure than money in the bank. He had been paying my storage bill in Nashville for over two years. I don't know of anyone else I could have counted on to do that without expecting something in return. Jasmine was always telling me to get over my hang-ups about not being attracted to him and run up to the altar with handcuffs on, but I couldn't do it.

"I'm going home next Friday to check on my family, can we do on Saturday?"

"I'll get a U-Haul, come by the house whenever and I'll be here."

"Thanks, Jason, I owe you big time."

***

I made the drive home to Pulaski in record time. I was so ready to get moved back into my own place again. I walked in the door and right away it didn't feel right to me. It was too quiet, and then I realized the TV was off. I couldn't remember it being off for more years than I cared to think about. Then my heart started to beat as the adrenaline from my fear rushed to it. Where was my mama?

"Mama, Mama," I shouted as I rushed to their bedroom.

She wasn't there and the bed was made as if no one had slept in it.

"Don't panic," I said to myself, clutching my chest to quiet my pounding heart, "Daddy probably took her with him to the store to get her out of the house."

I needed to stop tripping, somebody would have called me if there was anything wrong. I went in the kitchen to get a drink of water to wet my dry mouth. That's when I noticed there wasn't much in the refrigerator, so they were surely at the grocery store. I went back into the living room and sat down to wait. I hadn't planned on staying long. I just wanted to pick up some clothes and things I had at the house and head to Nashville to get the rest of my stuff out of storage. If they took much longer to get back home it was going to be a long day.

I was just about to lean my head back and close my eyes for a minute when I heard my daddy holler from the back door, "Tia, when did you get here?"

"Hey, Daddy," I said, rising to my feet and walking into the kitchen, "I got the apartment with my paycheck so I came home to get my stuff." Seeing him in the kitchen by himself without Mama in her wheel chair stopped me dead in my tracks. "Where's Mama?"

"Come on over and sit down, baby, I need to talk to you," he said, reaching his arm out to pull me closer to the table.

I moved over to him like a baby taking its first steps, "What's going on, where's Mama."

"Tia, your mama is fine, so hold your horses. She's staying in a long-term care facility about fifteen minutes from here."

"What are you telling me, Daddy? You moved Mama without talking to me or telling me about it. When did this happen?"

"I wanted to tell you, but I knew you wouldn't agree with what I had to do. You needed to go on with your life without worrying about us, that's why I didn't say anything to you. Your mama has been on a waiting list for five months, they called and said they had a space a week after you left."

Tears started to spill out of my eyes and poured down my face. I wasn't prepared for this. How could he have done this without me being here? I imagined how upset she was when he told her about it. I wondered if she had thrown a fit.

"Daddy, I appreciate you not wanting me to worry, but she's my mama. I want to be there for her when she needs me."

"She's my wife and I am the one who has to make the decisions for her. She's not going to get any better. I've got to go to work so that I can provide for her, you've got to work to take care of yourself, and Thomas has four kids and a new wife. I didn't have the time or energy to bathe her in the mornings, make all of her meals, and be here to make sure that she doesn't fall and hurt herself or try to cook and burn the house down."

"I told you that I would stay with her for a while longer. We could have put that off for a long time, Daddy. That was supposed to be the last resort."

"It wasn't something I wanted to do, Tia, it's what the doctors recommended. You were there when they told us we would have to consider putting her in a facility. The time came and now we have to accept it."

"It's kind of hard for me to accept that without you

208

considering that we had other options."

"Get your things together and put them in your car. When you get done I'll take you over to see her for yourself."

I got my television and boom-box and some other things I had come to get for my apartment and loaded them in my car even though I wasn't sure if I was going back at this point. I stopped by Mama and Daddy's bedroom and looked around. I almost broke down with the thought that maybe she wouldn't ever be coming back to the house again. I had put it out of my mind for a while but now it was back front and center. I was slowly but surely losing my mama.

"I want you to trail me in your car because you need to get moving after your visit," Daddy said sternly, as if I wasn't grown and had to listen to what he said.

I nodded my head, got into my car and started the engine. I followed close behind him and it made me feel like I was in a funeral procession. One part of me wanted to turn left when he turned right into the parking lot, drive off and not even face the situation, but there was no escaping it, my mama was living in some kind of nursing home. It looked all right from the outside but I starting praying that it didn't smell like urine when I walked in.

Daddy spoke to a nurse or technician dressed in scrubs at the front desk and she smiled at me when I passed. I took a deep breath and all I could smell was pine cleaner. I followed Daddy down two corridors and then three doors down until I saw her name, Samantha King, written in magic marker under the number 113 on the side of the door. Daddy pushed the door open and I could hear the television playing before I saw her sitting in her wheel chair by the window. I was surprised that she looked good, her hair was combed and she was dressed in a forest green velour jogging outfit. The room was bigger than theirs at home with a full size bed and a sitting area with a love seat and a rocking chair around a small coffee table.

"Honey, look who I brought to see you today," he said as we moved closer to where she was sitting.

She turned towards us and looked at me for a moment like she was confused.

"It's, Tia," he said, sitting down on the loveseat.

"Hi, Mama," I said, giving her a hug before I sat down in the rocking chair.

"Well, it's about damn time you got here," she said, leaning back in the wheel chair, "How long does it take for you to go to the store and bring me back my cigarettes."

"Mama, you quit smoking twenty years ago," I said, hoping she was playing a joke.

"Ain't that some shit. Look, child, if you don't have them, where the hell is my money?" she asked, getting more upset.

"Don't worry, honey," Daddy said to her, rubbing her on the arm, "I'll get them for you, Tia has been busy working at her new job."

"All right, that's good, I don't want her to get in trouble," she said, calming down.

Her attention drifted back to the television and then Daddy said, "Tia has got to go or she'll be late, honey."

"Okay, baby," she said as if she was her normal self, looking at me with those hurt puppy dog eyes that said take me with you.

Each step out of there was a knife in my heart and it was killing me to walk away. Yet I knew Daddy was right. Taking care of her at home was more than any one of us could handle. The mama I knew was slipping away. The truth was if I changed my plans and stayed with the person living here it wouldn't be five minutes before she'd be cussing me out thoroughly.

"You all right, baby girl?" Daddy asked when we got to my car.

"Yeah, I'm fine and I'm going back, but I don't want you to keep anything about Mama and her condition from me."

"I won't, I just wanted to give you a chance to get situated there on your job."

"I'm good now, Daddy," I said, giving him a tight hug that I hoped would keep his spirits up.

I got in my car and gave him another wave from the window before I sped off towards the interstate without looking back. I didn't want the sight of the building to be fixed in my mind. Why is it every time I get one end pulled together another piece falls apart?

***

"I was about to call you," Jason said when he answered the door, "I thought you had car trouble or something worse."

"It wasn't car trouble, but it was something worse. I don't want to talk about it right now or I won't be worth a quarter and we have a lot to do."

"Let's roll then, the U-haul is ready and waiting," he said, leading the way to the truck.

"Do you think we need to call anybody to help us get the

211

truck loaded?" I asked while he drove to the storage company. I was wondering if I had the strength to pull my own weight.

"I think we can handle it, the biggest things are your mattress and the sofa and I don't think we need help with those. You get on one side and I've got the other," he said, giving me a soft punch on the shoulder.

"If you only knew, Jason, I think you would make a phone call."

"Come on, Tia, we got this, besides we don't have a lot of time to wait for someone to get over here. Plus, whenever moving is involved most people are too busy to help."

"You're right," I said, reflecting back on my past moving experiences.

I thanked the Lord for Jason, without him I would be doing this move on my own. We pulled the truck in front of my storage unit and I got out and unlocked the door. Jason slid the door up and there were all my worldly goods neatly stacked in a 10'x10' unit. Here I was almost 37 years old and everything I've accumulated on this earth can fit it this cubicle.

Jason looked at all the boxes stacked to the ceiling and made a suggestion, "I think we should take the boxes out first and put them to the side, load up the large things and then set the boxes back on top."

"That sounds like a plan to me," I said, glad to follow his lead; the whole job was starting to overwhelm me.

It took us just over an hour to get everything out of the storage unit and loaded up in the U-haul truck. Jason figured that it would be easier if he trailed me to Atlanta in the truck and then drove it back to Nashville the next day. It was music to my ears. It would save me from another round-trip drive. On the road in the car alone my mind replayed the visit with Mama. She was so mean and cold towards me. It was more than I could think about so I dug out my Mary J. Blige CD to hear, "No More Drama", and let it play all the way to Atlanta.

"What is in all these boxes?" Jason asked after we got the last one in my new apartment.

"I've got a thing for small kitchen appliances," I answered with no apology, "I have all the latest mixers, mini-ovens, grills, bread makers, blenders, lettuce dryers, and whatever other kitchen gadget you can name. It's my main vice, I can't explain it."

We got the bed set up, the living room in place, and my kitchen table ready for company. I would deal with all the boxes later. My new home had taken shape and I was so happy, aside from the fact that Jason and I were so tired we could barely stand.

"There's a Chinese place near here that delivers, how's that sound?" I asked just before Jason collapsed on the floor in front of the sofa.

"That sounds good enough. After I catch my breath I'll hook up your television and DVD player. If you don't have any cable channels yet at least you can watch a movie."

"I don't know what I would do without you, Jason, you are my hero."

"You don't have to do without me, Tia, and I know you don't like to talk about it but I would do anything for you. I still wouldn't mind taking this to the next level and however far it could go. We get along great. I can even see us married if that's what you want."

"Let me order the food first because this is getting deep and I'm hungry," I said, avoiding the subject.

I looked in my phone directory and called the Chinese place. I ordered egg drop soup, two egg rolls, some barbeque ribs, two entrees, and some Chinese donuts. Jason loved to eat as much as I did. Through a heavy accent I got the total of $31.00 and a delivery time of 30 minutes. I walked over and sat down on the sofa next to Jason.

"You know we have had this conversation so many times," I said gently. "You may be my closest friend and I don't want to jeopardize that. You are more of a brother to me than Thomas."

"Friend is the other 'F' word, Tia. Are you still on that 'I'm not attracted to you like that' trip?"

"That's the bottom line, but not the whole story."

"How do you know if you're not attracted to me if we've never kissed?"

"I don't have to kiss you to know."

"If I didn't know you better I would think this is basically something racial."

"I'm sorry. I have never imagined myself with anyone else other than a black man. We all have our preferences. I don't fault you for your attraction to black women."

"I could love you better than any black man if you would let me."

"You probably could," I said just as the doorbell rang. Except I couldn't get over my hang-up.

The food was delicious and I knew that it would only be a matter of time before the heavy-accented woman who took my order over the phone and I would be on a first-name basis. I made a bed for Jason on the couch and I spent the first night in my apartment stretched out across the top of my bed too tired to undress or shower.

"Let's go out for breakfast," Jason said, pulling my hair and waking me up, "I'm going to have to get this truck back by 5:00 or they're going to charge me for another day."

Scrubbed and refreshed we found an I-HOP near the mall.

"I've decided that I want to take you on a weekend trip to Florida to thank you for taking care of my storage fees and helping me move," I said once we were seated at a table.

"Is this a "friend" trip?"

"Jason, why are you tripping on me? You're making me feel like the bad guy."

"I'm just asking because I might want to bring a date."

"Wow," I said, surprised at his response. "If that means that you will have a better time on the trip, then by all means bring a date."

For the rest of the meal we didn't do a lot of talking and Jason didn't waste any time getting in the U-Haul when we got back to the apartment. It was just like the Will Downing re-make of "I Can't Make You Love Me" where the lyrics say "I can't make my heart feel something that it won't." He had given me something to think about though, how do you really know if you're attracted to someone if you don't kiss? I watched the back of the truck until the sign saying $19.95 blurred and faded into the white paint and then I went back inside my apartment.

14

Chapter Fourteen

I wasn't ready to get into the huge job of unpacking my boxes yet. The first thing on my list was to go to Wal-Mart and pick up some food and cleaning supplies. I was shocked when this boy looking like he was in middle school came up to me in the frozen food section.

"Excuse me, are you married?" he asked, looking up at me.

"No, I'm not," I answered, wondering what it was all about.

"Do you have a boyfriend?"

"No, I don't and where is your mama or daddy?"

"Would it be possible for me to get your phone number?"

I couldn't believe my ears, was this some type of set-up?

"No, little boy," I said, pushing my cart away from him, "I just moved here and I'm not interested."

I couldn't stop shaking my head while I finished my shopping. A young boy had the nerve to step to me. I was probably old enough to be his mama. Standing in line I thought there was nothing else that could happen that day that could amaze me. I was rolling out of the store when this brother stopped walking and stood in front of my path.

"Excuse me, miss, but I know I couldn't forget that face," he said, moving beside me.

Here we go again. Is the insanity in the water or in the air? Once he stepped to the side I started rolling again, I wasn't in the mood for hearing another pick-up line. Then I stopped, I thought that maybe I knew his face too.

I turned around and said, "What the hell, oh my God, Earnest."

"It's a small world, Tia," he said, smiling, "But right now I'm loving it."

"What are you doing in Atlanta?" I asked, still stunned by seeing him.

"I've been here for two or three years now. What are you doing here?"

"I'm working."

"That's tight," he said, nodding his head. "Let me help you get your stuff to your car."

I moved over so he could push the cart while I tried to shake off the shock of seeing him. I had met Earnest on MySpace about six years ago. He wasn't a baller or had a college degree and I didn't think we had anything to talk about. I didn't think he was good enough for me to talk to, but after I got played so many times my standards were lowered.

He told me he was thirty years old and we chatted for a few months before he came to meet me at school. That's when I found out that he had a baby-mama and had lied about his age; he was actually seven and a half years younger. We started to hang out even though age is more than a number to me, he was eight years younger than I was. We liked the same things and spent a lot of time together, I even introduced him to my mama. He loved to buy me roses to put on my desk in the lab. We broke up a year later when I found out he was engaged to his baby-mama.

I had barely recognized him, he was cute back then, not so much now, he had gained a lot of weight. I opened the trunk and he loaded all my things in the back.

"Thank you," I said when he was finished, "I moved here for a job about six weeks ago and I'm just getting settled in my apartment."

"I don't want to hold you up but I'd like to get your number."

I gave him my cell number and he put it in his cell phone, then he gave me his.

That was strange. Who would expect to run into somebody you dated in another city? My love-life was out of control. Reggie had sent me another text that his job was definitely moving to Nashville within the month. One reason I had put Reggie down was because I didn't want a long distance relationship and now that we were in the same town he was moving. Now I run into a guy I hadn't seen in years walking into Wal-Mart.

I couldn't wait to get home and locate the box with my photo album in it. Earnest looked so different that I had to refresh my memory of what he used to look like. I flipped through the pages until I saw the picture we had taken together.

"It's an omen," I said to myself. The date of the picture were the same date as today, it couldn't be a coincidence.

I picked up my phone and texted him, "It was good to see you today."

He texted me back, "I'm glad I went to the store when I did, you still look good."

We texted back and forth all week and on Friday he asked, "Do you wanna get a drink?"

We met at an Applebee's near the campus. I stared out the window of the restaurant when I saw him get out of his pick-up truck. He was kind of hefty when we were talking years ago, but now he looked like he was over 450 pounds. I know I'm a big girl and I shouldn't judge but this was taking it to another level.

He saw me when he came through the door and walked over to the table. When he squeezed in the booth the table was hard pressed between the two of us. I tried to smile and made a mental note that if we went out again we should sit at a table instead of a booth. We talked a lot, catching up on what's been going on in our lives over the past four years. It had been a busy week so I cut the evening short with him agreeing to stop by my place on Saturday to put my media chest together for me.

***

"Nice area," he said when I opened the door.

"A female living alone has to be careful," I said as he walked in looking around.

"I haven't had a chance to eat yet, what do you have in the fridge?" he asked, making his way towards my kitchen.

"All I have in there is some left over pizza that I was going to have for my dinner." I answered.

He pulled out the box, looked in my cabinets for a plate, and proceeded to warm the pizza up in the microwave. I was speechless that he would have this much nerve after I told him I planned to eat it myself. I was making a little money but this sister was still on a budget.

"Where's this thing you need to have put together?" he asked between bites.

"It's over here," I said, agitated as I led him back into the living room and pointed at the box sitting in the middle of the floor.

I started pulling the large pieces out of the box and the bags of screws and arranged them on the floor according to the directions.

"Let me do this," he said, raising his hands, "Sit back and let me be the man."

He got down on the floor, looked at the picture on the outside of the box for a few seconds, and then started putting the pieces together without reading directions. I could see he was getting ready to fuck up my shit.

"I would prefer if you followed the procedure given on the papers provided," I said angrily, unable to hold my tongue for another minute, especially after he had polished off my dinner without even offering me any.

"Why don't you sit down and watch some TV or call one of your girlfriends until I get finished with this. Trust me; I know what I'm doing."

It was my fault for asking him to help, so I went over and turned the TV on and resigned myself to live with whatever mess he made out of my entertainment center. What was wrong with me? Yesterday I was ready to say he was the one just because of a date on a picture. I could hear my mama's words ringing out clearly in my head, "Tia, are you that desperate?"

I leaned back against the sofa and closed my eyes. When I opened them an hour later I was pleasantly surprised to find that by some miracle he had put the chest together and it looked really nice. He had pushed it up against the wall and connected my music player, DVD player, and TV, all in their places.

"Thank you, that was a big help, and I'm sorry for criticizing and interfering with your mechanical flow."

"Not a problem, I understand," he said, "I needed to make you a believer."

"I'll admit that you have me convinced, at least for now," I said, happy that the job was over and I didn't have to raise any hell.

"I've got some other things to do, Tia, I'm getting my grind on today. Do you want me to stop back by when I get done?"

"Don't worry about it, I'm going over to work in the lab for a while and it'll probably be late when I get back. I'll be in touch."

I walked him to the door and he raised his hand up for a high five. I smiled and gave him a soft slap. I stood in the doorway with dismay as I watched his body wobble and jiggle over to his car. I wanted to make sure he was out of the parking lot before I called Jasmine.

"I have got some news for you," I told her as soon as she answered.

"Oh let me sit down, I think I hear wedding bells," she said, being funny.

"No, it's not that serious but I did run into somebody I hadn't seen in a long time when I was at Wal-Mart. Do you remember me talking about a guy named Earnest?"

"Honey, your list is so long I can't keep track of the names."

"Don't give me a hard time, he's and old friend that I met during my first year."

"So what does he do and how did he end up in Atlanta?"

"He doesn't have a career, he said he came down here to go to school."

"What does he do to put food on the table?"

"He says that he moves furniture, sells knock-off purses, and he cuts hair."

"That's a lot for one man, he sounds like he's a little hustler."

"He's not little."

"What do you mean? Is he tall or heavy?"

"Heavy, and I mean heavy. I know I have changed some too, but he is twice the man he was when I saw him last."

"Well, what do you have on your mind? Are you thinking about getting into something with him, or is he going to be just a friend?"

"I like him, we've had a couple of long conversations and he's real deep, and he was real patient when I gave him much attitude. I wouldn't mind spending some time with him but I don't want to be intimate with him. I totally agree with my favorite comedian, Bruce Bruce, two big people don't need to get together."

"I don't know what to tell you girl, I know how your mind works when it comes to dating. Every time you meet a man you feel like its divine intervention. Sometimes it's just about saying hello and keeping it moving."

"I'm like that because I don't want to take a chance on missing the person I'm supposed to be with."

"I think you should change your whole philosophy and put this obsession of getting married out of your mind for a while. I'm starting to agree with your mama, you are getting desperate. Call her and I bet she'll tell you the same."

"I'm scared to call her. She might start cussing me out or worse, she might not even know who I am."

***

I definitely needed to increase the number of men in the pool I had to choose from and the late night commercial for blackworld.com inspired me to join the domain of online dating. I meticulously set up my profile as the professional African-American woman looking to meet someone with similar likes and ambitions. My picture was one I had taken about three years ago at my graduation. I was happy and smiling and thirty-seven pounds lighter. In less than forty-eight hours I had three hits of eligible employed black men. If this were a game of baseball, all the bases would be loaded. Now all I needed was for one of them to be the special one I had been waiting for and make my house into a home.

Wanting to keep my options open, I started chatting with all three, Randy, Earl, and Darnell. I loved the attention, it made me feel like it was freshman year in college again. I met Randy first. He was forty-two years old, a former Greyhound bus driver on disability. He posted a headshot showing none of his physique, so that made me a bit suspicious, but he was dark-skinned the way I like them with a cute face and dimples. He lived about 100 miles from me but he was coming into Atlanta for a basketball tournament and wanted to meet me. I arranged to meet him on campus after work on Friday.

The mystery of the headshot was solved when he got out of the car, he looked like Sponge Bob's sidekick, Patrick. His chest and stomach were meshed into one humongous mound of flesh with twig legs sticking out from under it. "I'm not a small girl, but damn!" He trailed me home and when he didn't mention taking me out to dinner I made some snacks for us to munch on. As much as he talked on the phone, once we were together he didn't have much to say. He was boring me to sleep to say the least. After a while I got up to get an early start on my Saturday chores.

"Relax and make yourself at home," I said, handing him the TV remote.

I cleaned the kitchen and loaded the dishwasher, changed my bed sheets, and then I separated the dirty clothes in my hamper.

"What are you doing?" he yelled out to me thirty minutes later.

"I'm putting a load in," I shouted back.

"When do I get to put a load in?" he asked, trying to sound sexy.

"LOL, that was funny," I said, adding detergent in the washing machine.

I shook my head in disgust, that was never going to happen. I've got too much meat, he's got too much meat, and that's not sexy.

"What hotel are you staying in?" I asked, dropping a huge hint.

"I was thinking I could stay with you this weekend," he answered.

"No way, I don't know you and you don't know me. That's how people come up missing."

"I know that was probably asking too much too soon."

"Extremely," I said in a huff, "Where do they do that?"

He finally left a few minutes later and I promptly deleted his number out of my phone. I lost count of the strikes against him, he was assuredly out.

The next day I called Earl. He was a forty-five year old accountant, not cute, but he owned his own home and two cars. He loved to talk and complained nonstop about his ex-wife and his seventeen year old son. Whenever I asked him when we were going to meet he would say after tax season was over. I didn't get it at first, why doesn't he want to hook-up. Through our many conversations I determined that he was stingy as hell and dating over the phone is as cheap as it gets. Needless to say he struck out too. I didn't need a phone pal.

Darnell was my last chance for winning the on-line love lottery. He was thirty-seven years old, a mechanic, and a cute guy. He's from New York and his conversation has an edge to it but when he talks about kissing me I get butterflies.

"I need to tell you that I dance part-time," he said in one of our talks over the phone.

"Are you telling me I'm talking to a stripper?" I asked offhandedly.

"That's right, my stage name is Horse. I can't even wear sweat pants because my print will show. I easily make $550 in a night."

I pause to swallow before I choked. "I know I can't deal with you. I'm not about that life."

"Don't get me wrong, Tia, I'm looking for somebody, for real for real. That's why I went on-line. I can't find a girl who will date a stripper or even take me seriously."

"If you're trying to get sympathy from me, don't waste your time."

"So it's like that," he said with resignation.

"And that's the way it is," I said, hanging up the phone.

So much for me finding the man of my dreams on-line. I called Jasmine to give her the latest update of my quest.

"I'm done with finding my future husband on the internet, girl, the score is zero out of three," I said as soon as she said hello.

"What happened to Darnell? You said you were saving the best for last."

"He's a stripper."

"Are you talking about Magic Mike type of stuff?" she asked, surprised.

"Yes, exactly, telling me his stage name is Horse."

"I'm glad you didn't go there, Tia, you can't date him. Nobody wants to be bothered with no horse."

"I beg to differ, Jazz, if I wasn't looking for something more I would have jumped on that horse."

"No way, the next thing you know you'd be having all kinds of female problems."

"My biggest problem is that I prefer to be involved with a southern gentleman."

"Child, what are you tripping on? I've been in the south for twenty years and I have yet to meet a southern gentleman."

"It doesn't matter, I'm done with all three of them, game over."

***

Against my better judgment, after my online dating fiasco I continued to see Earnest, I guess being with him was better than being alone for me right now. He never takes me anywhere, never has any money, and he's always eating up whatever food I need to ration out for myself. I knew the relationship wasn't going anywhere when I took him to the lab one night with me to complete an experiment and two of my lab mates were there working. There was no way out of introducing him and it was then I realized I was embarrassed for people to think he was my man.

He added insult to injury one weekend when he stood me up as my date to a co-workers birthday party with a feeble explanation about being at a church program. I had the unmistakable feeling that he was trying to play me. The question is; who is the other woman out there, who as my mama would say, is desperate as I am, since he can't afford to date one woman much less two.

15

Chapter Fifteen

Somehow I had adjusted to all the changes in my life over the last four months. I re-gained some momentum in my research at work, my apartment was all unpacked and organized, but I was missing home. Mother's Day was coming up and I had to go and see my mama, I didn't know if she missed me, but I was missing her more than I had in all my life. Up to her getting sick, she had always been there for me. I called my Daddy and told him I was coming home on the weekend.

He was washing his truck on the drive way when I pulled up in front of the house on Saturday night. "Hey Daddy," I said, rushing over to him to give him a hug, "I missed y'all."

"Hey, baby girl, I missed you too," he said, putting down the hose to hug me back.

"How's Mama doing?" I asked when he bent down to pick the hose back up.

"She's doing all right, I told her you were coming for a visit for Mother's Day."

"What time are we going over to the facility in the morning?" I asked as he dried the excess water from the truck. I still refused to let the words 'nursing home' cross my lips.

"I'm not going with you, Tia. I think you need some time alone with her. I don't want her to feel uncomfortable with me there."

"What are you talking about?" I asked, confused.

"Sometimes she can be irritable and I don't want anything to spoil your visit. We can go out to dinner together later when you come home."

"Okay, Daddy," I said, grabbing my weekend bag and going in the house.

I put the bag down in my bedroom and came back out into the living room and turned on the TV. I sat down in the recliner where my mama had spent so much time sitting and tried to imagine how the world looked from her eyes. I was facing the TV but my thoughts were focused in another direction. I tried to fathom how she felt knowing that one day she wouldn't be herself, that she wouldn't remember her own past or recognize the members of her family. That would be an overwhelming thing to deal with and suddenly I understood her anger and frustration.

I woke up early the next morning still in her chair and the TV still on. It was the smell of bacon that had lulled me awake, Daddy knew it was one of my favorite foods. I took a quick shower and put on one of my mama's dresses that she kept in her closet even though they had been too small for nearly fifteen years. I put on a pair of her dressy low-heeled sandals and found some of her jewelry that matched. I needed to have some things of hers next to me as a comfort just in case she didn't remember me. Daddy was already gone so I threw a handful of bacon between two slices of bread, took a bottle of orange juice out of the fridge, and headed over to the facility.

"I'm here to see Mrs. King," I told a young woman at the front desk and then I suddenly wished I had brought flowers or a gift or something.

"She's in the chapel, they're having a special service for Mother's Day. You can go on back, it's the first door on your left after you go through the double doors."

"Thank you," I told her, following her directions.

My nervousness started playing havoc with the bacon sandwich and orange juice as I got closer to the door. I pushed it in slowly not to disturb the service inside. On the right I saw my mother sitting in a wheel chair with her legs raised at the end of the second row and there was an empty chair beside her. I tiptoed around the back and up the side and eased across her chair and sat down. She looked at me and the recognition in her eyes was like a cool drink of water to a woman who had been lost in the desert.

"Hey, Mama," I whispered as I gave her a side hug.

"Tia," she said, squeezing my hand and smiling at me.

We both listened as the pastor spoke about the depths and expanse of a mother's love, saying, *"No matter what turmoil may cloud or shake our existence, that love remains pure and intact."* I wrapped my fingers around hers and it was the sweetest moment that I can remember us sharing.

When the service was over I stood up to push her chair.

"Do you want to go outside and get some fresh air?" I asked.

"That sounds nice," she answered. "You look so pretty I want to take your picture."

On the way out to the courtyard they had for their patients

and their families I stopped to speak with the young woman from the front desk.

"Would you take a picture of my mother and me?"

"Sure, do you want to take it right here or do you want to take it outside?"

"I'd love to take it outside, it's such a pretty day," I replied.

The truth was I didn't want a picture of us inside the building. Even though they seemed to take good care of her, I still felt guilty about her being there. I handed the young woman my cell phone once we were out of the door.

"Stand beside me, Tia, I want your dress in the picture."

I stood as close to her as I could get and the young woman took the picture.

"Could you take another one close up?" I asked as I kneeled down where our cheeks almost touched.

"That was a good one," she said, handing me my phone and going back inside.

I saw a perfect spot in the shade at the edge of the courtyard where there were some chairs and a table. I wheeled Mama towards the area and the chair glided over the thick lawn.

"I missed you, Mama, how are you doing?" I asked as soon as I got her positioned and took a seat across from her.

"My legs are giving me fits but other than that I'm doing good."

"Are they treating you all right here, because if they're not, I'll take you out of here today."

"The people here are real nice, I don't have no complaints. The food ain't so hot but it'll do and I get to watch all my favorite shows."

"Do you miss me, Mama? We don't get to talk much like we used to."

"All you got to do is call me, I'm here and I ain't going nowhere."

"I know that but I feel bad that I'm not the one taking care of you."

"Girl, you can barely take care of yourself, how you gonna take care of me? I don't want to be a burden on my family, go on and live your life. I bet you got some worthless nigger you sneaking around with."

I smiled to myself, this was vintage, Mama was back and sitting in front of me today. It was Mother's Day for real.

"Does that mean you're not going to dance at my wedding?" I asked, reviving an old joke between us.

"I'll be there, but it might not be anything to dance about," she said, laughing. "Getting older has gotten you desperate."

I shook my head, she was right. There was no way I could tell her that I had been so desperate that I had let Earnest climb his big ass on me with the weight of his stomach on my back and mount me like the bull did to the cow on my Uncle Nathan's farm.

"No, Mama, I'm not seeing anybody right now and today I have decided to be in love with me, myself, and I, like Beyonce said, 'I'm gonna be my own best friend.'"

"I'm glad to hear that because life isn't all about a man."

"Mama, weren't you crazy about Daddy when you first met him?"

"No I wasn't, my mama taught me that a woman should marry a man that loves her more than she loves him."

That was one lesson that she hadn't been able to teach me and I wasn't so sure if that was the kind of relationship I wanted. It seemed to me that she had missed out on getting love from my Daddy by refusing to give it to him. That wasn't real happiness as far as I had seen. We sat for a few minutes enjoying the intermittent breeze that blew across the courtyard.

"Lunchtime," a voice called from the entrance.

"Mama, do you want me to stay and eat lunch with you?" I asked.

"Did you bring me the cigarettes?" she asked indignantly.

"No, Mama, I forgot them," I answered, seeing that the precious moment we shared had been fleeting.

"Oh hell, where's my money then, I'll get them myself."

"I'll get them for you, Mama," I said, rolling her chair back inside to the dining room, "Right now it's time to eat lunch."

"Will you be coming back later?" the young woman at the front entrance asked as I waved my hand on the way out.

"No, I think she was getting a little tired."

I got in my car feeling more at peace with the situation than I had since her diagnosis. It was what it was. All in all, it had been a good day. I drove by the house and since Daddy wasn't there I left him a note and headed back on the drive to Atlanta.

By the time I got in town my stomach was grumbling above the volume of the radio. I don't know why but I had a taste for some spaghetti. I detoured to the Publix grocery store that was about a mile from my apartment complex to get the ingredients for my own special meat sauce recipe. I reached for the Angus ground beef. My new philosophy was to be good to myself, so I was worth the extra money per pound over the ground chuck.

When I got home I changed into an over-sized t-shirt and

headed into the kitchen to get my show on the road. I put on a pot of water to boil for the pasta. I got out a skillet to brown the ground Angus for the meat sauce. Then the mellow groove I was on went up in smoke. The beautiful red meat I had purchased at $4.89 per pound was gray inside.

My tastes buds were already fired up so I cut away the red part and made enough sauce for one serving. The rest of that meat was going back to the grocery store for a full refund as soon as I got off work. I may be slightly hypersensitive but I don't like to be taken advantage of.

I kept the meat in the lab refrigerator because I knew the experiment I was working on would keep me there until at least 6:30. On my way out I was so anxious to get to the store that I was halfway to my car before I realized I hadn't gotten the meat out of the fridge. That only made me more irritated as I doubled back on my aching feet. I was in my hell-raising mode for sure. It was only the fact that rush hour traffic had begun to clear that calmed me down on my way back to Publix.

I walked straight to the customer service desk and dropped the meat on the counter. A college-age girl wearing a name tag that said, 'Hello, my name is Mandy' came over to help me.

"Hi, I bought this meat yesterday and when I got home it was all gray inside," I said, courteously.

She looked down at the mess lying on the counter and asked, "Do you have your receipt?"

I searched around in my purse and it wasn't there. It must still be in one of the Publix bags at home in my recycle drawer.

"No, I'm sorry I don't, I must have left it at home in another bag," I replied.

"There's no way for me to know what day this meat was purchased and it looks like the package has a good amount of meat missing," she said in a condescending tone. "Would you like to speak with the manager?"

"Yes, please," I said politely, I didn't feel like going off in here and showing these people that I don't play about my money.

I stood at the counter gazing at past winning lotto numbers wondering if I would have played any of the numbers there when I heard a deep voice come up behind me.

"Hello, I'm the manager, ma'am, is there a problem I can help you with?"

"Yes I bought this higher cut of meat here yesterday and it wasn't fresh and I would like to have a refund. I don't have my receipt but the label there says how much I paid for it," I said, trying not to get upset before I had to.

"I'm sorry about that, ma'am; we pride ourselves on the quality of our meat. If I can see your driver's license I will gladly replace the ground beef for you or give you a store credit if that will make you happy."

"Yes, that would make me happy," I said, smiling with relief that I wouldn't have to go ghetto on anybody this evening.

"I don't think I introduced myself, my name is Michael Goodwin," he said, reaching out for a handshake, "As a bonus I will add two of our premium steaks as an apology for your dissatisfaction. I would even cook them for you and I'm a good cook if you would consider it."

Did I hear him correctly? Was he offering to cook dinner for me? I was so caught up in the funk I was prepared to raise that I hadn't even really looked at the manager. Taking a quick glance I saw he was a tall, clean cut, milk chocolate brother with nice arm muscles, probably from lifting boxes and stocking shelves. He was a little thick around the waist, not a huge belly, just enough to let you know he liked to eat.

"That sounds like a great offer but the store credit is fine, I don't want to take advantage of the situation," I said, being cordial.

"You wouldn't be," he insisted, "It's the least I can do. I see that you are from out of town. I wouldn't want to give a visitor the wrong impression about our city."

"Actually I just moved here, I'm doing research at the university."

"Then you are going to have to let me welcome you to Atlanta properly."

"You are one day short, I just swore off men yesterday."

"I think you should give me your number, you might change your mind by the weekend," he said, smiling.

"All right," I said, writing it on the back of my return receipt, "I might get hungry for premium steaks and I'm on a budget."

I smiled all the way home. It felt good to be asked but I wasn't interested. Michael was a nice-looking guy who was gainfully employed but I was going to stay seated on the sideline for a while, I was tired of playing the game. The only thing I was open for was solitaire. Although it was nice to know I could still get some attention.

I was under the fume hood working in the lab on Thursday when my cell phone, tucked in the chest pocket of my lab coat, vibrated against my breast. A few minutes later I looked and it was a text message from my friendly manager from the neighborhood Publix, Michael.

It said, "The weekend is fast approaching and the steaks are marinating. Say you'll let me prepare your TGIF dinner. Your place or mine?"

I didn't have any plans and the weather was so beautiful. I broke down and texted him back, "I'd hate for those premium steaks to go to waste. Give me your address and the time dinner will be served and I'll be there."

He didn't respond and then bad thoughts filled my head, he was probably married or living with someone, those were the only kind that were attracted to me. I brushed it off as no harm done. I could always order in some Chinese food and watch some TV.

I was running late the next morning and when my phone starting ringing I knew it was Marissa checking to see if I was coming in. I grabbed the cell and pushed talk and was about to tell her I was on my way when I heard the deep male voice.

"Tia, I didn't get your text last night, my phone battery died while I was working and I didn't get it charged until this morning. I'm glad you decided to accept my offer."

"You know how I am about letting prime beef go to waste."

"I can bring the meal over to your place if you like, I live outside the perimeter?"

"No, that's okay; if you're doing the cooking I don't mind the drive."

"All right, I'll text you my address and you can put it in your GPS."

"Okay, what time should I be there?"

"Is 7:00 too early?"

"No, that's perfect," I said, "I'll see you later then."

I spent the rest of the drive to work trying to decide if I had made another desperate move or not. By the time I pulled into my parking spot I figured that I hadn't. I was only going to dinner. What was wrong with getting to know some people outside of work, after all this was my new home. More to the point, Michael was probably just being friendly.

"What are you doing this weekend?" Marissa asked, grinning from ear to ear when she came into the lab towards the end of the day. "The spring semester is over and most of the students are taking a break."

"I'm having dinner with a friend," I said, not wanting to go into any details.

"Well, I haven't said too much about it because I didn't want to make a big fuss but Carlos and I got engaged on New Year's Day and we're going to Gatlinburg to get married in one of the chapels. Would you like to drive up with us and be my bridesmaid?"

I wanted to use the words of the late great Whitney Houston and say, "Hell to the naw," but I serenely replied, "I would have loved to if I had known sooner, but this friend is from out of town."

"I'm disappointed but I understand. Anyway I'm leaving early since tomorrow is my wedding day and I've got things to do. I'll see you next week."

I picked up a journal off of my desk to fan myself, my adrenaline was pumping overtime. I had just dodged a bullet, maybe even a torpedo. I owed it all to Michael and his invitation. On the way home to change, I picked up a bottle of Merlot to take to the dinner and celebrate.

Chapter Sixteen

I had taken my shower over a half hour ago and I still didn't know what to wear. I didn't want to wear blue jeans, I didn't want to look like I was going to work, and I definitely didn't want to look like I was going to church. One thing was clear I needed to buy some new clothes. Back deep in the closet I found a maxi dress, it was jersey with diagonal stripes, and made like a tank top above the waist. I slipped it on and thank God it fit. I slipped on some low-heel sandals, put on light make-up, picked out my hair, and grabbed the bottle of wine on the way out.

The GPS said it would be 30 minutes to my arrival time. To me that was a long drive to get to the address Michael gave me but that's how it is in Atlanta. I hadn't learned much of the city streets since I had been there, mostly I went to work and shopped in my neighborhood. Thirty minutes later, moving off the highway, I followed the directions to a quiet street in Lawrenceville where the crape myrtle trees were lush and full and sprinkled with the colors of pink, red, and white. I followed the addresses on the neat mailboxes until I came to 3208. It was a very nice home and the grass was freshly cut.

"Welcome, come on in," Michael said when he opened the door, "You look very nice this evening."

"Thank you," I said, handing him the bottle of wine, "You look nice yourself."

I didn't say that to be nice. Michael looked like a different man without his red Publix smock on. He was wearing a lightweight cream colored knit shirt with black jeans. I couldn't help but give this man a second look as I followed him into the kitchen. My favorite cologne, Irish Spring Soap wafted in the air behind him.

"You didn't have to bring anything," he said, putting the wine on the counter.

"I know, my mama told me never to come to a dinner empty-handed."

"She sounds like my mama," he said, smiling.

"You have a very nice home," I said, looking around the kitchen and into the family room.

"Thanks, I got a good price on it when the housing market tanked during the recession."

"You seem like such a together brother, you have a good job, a home of your own, you don't mind doing the cooking, so I have to ask are you married or seeing someone?"

"Neither," he answered with a chuckle, "Come on and eat before my feast gets cold."

He pulled out a chair for me to sit in the small dining room off of the kitchen. The table was already set complete with cloth napkins. He had class too.

"I don't want to sound out of order and you will find that I'm a pretty blunt person but I have to ask what is wrong with you?"

"What do you mean?" he asked with a smile on his face as he set the food on the table.

"I mean, what is your fatal flaw, do you have a mental illness, a health condition, ten children, on the down-low, what is your story?"

"Tia, what you see is who I am. I'm not crazy, I'm not sick, I don't have any children, and I'm not complicated. I've had a few serious relationships but I don't want anybody who wants to be with me just because I have a paycheck or a roof over my head. I have my standards for what I'm looking for in a lady."

"I can understand that, I feel the same way and to show my good manners I'll bless the food."

I said a short prayer and then Michael popped the cork on the bottle wine. He served two thick porterhouse steaks, scalloped potatoes, French green beans, and a fresh salad with mandarin oranges in it. I was impressed, it all looked and smelled delicious.

"Get comfortable and enjoy your meal because it's my turn to give you the third degree," Michael said as I lifted my fork.

"I don't know if I can talk and eat at the same time."

"There's no rush, its Friday night, no work tomorrow."

"Not exactly, I do work some weekends," I said.

"Maybe it's time to tell me about yourself and what you do for a living."

"I work as a post-doctorate fellow in a research lab at University of Georgia. I've only been in town about six months, I moved here from a small town outside of Nashville where I was staying with my parents while I looked for a job. I have one brother, two nieces, and two nephews. I have never been married and I don't have any children. That should answer most of your questions."

"Not by a long shot but that was a good start," he said, taking a bite of the steak.

"Even so, that's more than I know about you," I responded.

"I'll take another turn, I don't mind. Both of my parents have passed away and I have two brothers and one sister. I don't know how many nieces and nephews I have, my brothers claim some and some they don't. I graduated from Atlanta Metropolitan College with a two-year degree in business management. I have been employed at my present job for eleven years."

"Would you mind if I asked you how old you are?" I said between a tender morsel of the steak.

"Not at all, I'm 48 years old," he said, taking another bite of food and a sip of wine.

Ten years were between us. I have always been fixated on age and not wanting a man much older or younger than myself. My rationale for this position is that similar age contributes to a better matched relationship, mentally as well as sexually.

"Is age a major factor for you in relationships?" he asked.

"Yes, it has been in the past," I answered, reflecting back over all the men I've dated.

"How has that worked out for you?" he asked curiously.

"Not very well I have to admit."

"Then maybe that's not the most important factor to look at. For me, I think that a person's family is a more important factor. It's who they are and how they've been raised that makes a difference."

"What do you mean?" I asked, finishing up my plate and reaching for another sip of wine, this conversation was getting deeper by the minute.

"It's all about having an example of a successful relationship to learn from and carry to the relationships that we have with other people.

Michael was surprising me more by the minute. He was mature, past the point of just trying to get a quick piece. He hadn't settled, he was a good man and he wanted a good woman. It was a bit intimidating. It wasn't what I was used to. I had never met anybody who made me question myself, I had always felt superior to the ones I had dated. I had been thinking the choice was all mine. Now I had to wonder if I had passed his test.

"I don't know if you're looking to get in a relationship but what kind of woman interests you?" I asked, almost afraid to hear his reply.

"Like most men, I like an attractive lady, but she has to be smart, proud, employed, motivated, neat, and most of all, easy to get along with. What about you, what are you looking for in a man?"

I took a moment to think, I hadn't looked for any specific qualities in the men I had been with besides physical attraction. I hadn't held them to any specific standard. I thought I wasn't settling but looking back I had more often than not.

After thinking about it I said, "Like most women, I like a tall, dark, and handsome man, but he has to be employed, educated, trustworthy, dependable, and frankly, sexually attracted to me."

"You took it there," he said, smiling.

"You were keeping it real so I followed your lead."

"Let's take this to another room," he said, refilling our glasses and carrying them with him.

In his den we sat down on the sofa and he turned on some music.

"I didn't mean to get into a heavy conversation on our first dinner," he said, facing me, "But I don't want to waste your time or mine. You have everything I'm looking for in a lady and I'm everything you mentioned that you wanted in a man. I would like to see you again and see where it takes us."

"I thought I was coming over for a casual meal and you have totally taken me by surprise. I'm usually going into things too quickly and regretting them later so I need to pump my brakes."

"That's cool, but I'm not looking for someone to date, been there and done that, I'm looking for someone who I can have a future with."

"I've been feeling like that since I graduated from high school and it only led me to make a bunch of bad decisions."

"I've seen your driver's license, Tia, I know how old you are. I'm ready to make a commitment and you are too."

This man didn't play, he was a take-charge kind of guy and I was from a household where my mother ruled the roost. I had to think about whether my upbringing, my trust issues, and my lack of genuine respect for men in general, which was influenced by my mother, would always cause me problems in a relationship.

"Honestly, I would like to get to know you," I said, standing on my feet and picking up my purse, "My hesitation is that I'm unlucky in love."

"You haven't met the right guy," he said, walking me to the door, "I might be the one to change all that."

"I enjoyed the dinner and the food for thought," I said, giving him a church hug.

Even after the long drive back to my apartment I was still shell-shocked. I didn't see this one coming. Michael had blown my mind. I hadn't met anybody like him and I didn't know how to react. Like he said, he was everything I was looking for in a man, but instead of jumping the gun and heading off to the races, I was scared. I didn't want to take a chance and then come out a loser again. I had promised myself that I was going to stay out of the game for a while.

I couldn't fall asleep thinking about the conversation I had with Michael over dinner. It was open and honest, what more did I want? I still had my hang-up about hooking up with an older man, what if he couldn't hang? Then there was the part when he talked about my age. That bullet went straight to the heart. Even so, it was true, I wasn't the PYT or the tenderoni anymore. I didn't know if it was too late but I reached for my phone.

"Hello, it's me, Tia," I said when he answered, "I wanted to tell you that I want to see you again."

"How about tomorrow, we can go see a movie," Michael said without hesitation.

"I'd like that, maybe we can meet somewhere halfway between us."

"I'll give you a call when I get it worked out," he said and then hung up.

This was different, a man making plans for me. I liked it.

What was wrong with becoming friends? I made a conscious decision not to tell anyone until we made it through thirty days of knowing each other.

I was so excited I couldn't sleep. I couldn't wait for the sun to rise so the new day would begin. I had so much to do. I washed my hair and headed to the nail shop a couple of blocks away. I could get a mani and a pedi while I waited for the mall to open.

My timing was on point so far, I was done at 10:05 and driving across the street to the Dress Barn to get a new outfit. I found the perfect ensemble. It was celery green, a loose fitting top over loose fitting pants. It was cool and comfortable the way I wanted to feel on my date with Michael.

The phone rang just as I got back home.

"Tia, I'm sorry, I'm going to have to give you a rain check on our date. Its Memorial Day weekend and several of my people have called in and we're shorthanded at the store. I'm going to have to go in."

"It happens, I understand," I said, disappointed.

"I'll call you back when I get a minute."

"Sure, no problem," I said, hanging up the phone with my hopes for a good weekend soon to go up in barbecue smoke.

But it was a problem. I had done exactly what I said I wouldn't do. I had gotten carried away only to be let down. I have been through too many relationship disappointments and I couldn't do it anymore. The best thing for me will be to let this go now before I let my emotions take control and I ended up looking like Boo Boo the Fool again.

Michael kept his word and called me but I didn't answer. For a week I refused to take his calls or answer his texts. I put all my time and energy into my work in the lab and I was getting some promising data. It was a sign that I had made the right decision. Another week passed and Michael had stopped calling.

***

Me, myself, and I spent Friday night on the sofa watching 'happily ever afters' on the Lifetime channel surrounded my real true loves, a bag of Lays potato chips, peanut M&Ms, and sweet tea. I woke up groggy the next morning from my private party and on my way to the bathroom I noticed a group of Jehovah Witnesses canvassing the complex and it was barely 9:00. It wouldn't be long before I had company. When I heard them knock I shuffled across the floor to politely tell them that I was a washed in the blood Baptist.

"Michael," was all I could say when I saw him on the other side of the door.

To say I was surprised to see him would be a colossal understatement, I thought he had moved on. Then the heat of embarrassment started to burn. I had answered the door in a raggedy faded oversized t-shirt without a bra. I hadn't combed my hair, washed my face, or brushed my teeth.

"I didn't want to show up at your door unannounced but you won't answer any of my calls," he said, standing there like a process server, "I got your address off of your driver's license the day we met."

"I did some thinking and re-initiated my boycott of men," I said as I tried to cover myself with the door.

"Uh-huh, well, I said I would take you to the movies and that's why I'm here," he said, stepping inside. "Take your time, get yourself together, I'll wait."

I was stunned and my mind was blank, I couldn't think of anything that would point him to a quick exit. There was no need for false pretenses, he had caught me off guard, and my likeness was unfiltered and untouched. I had learned another hard lesson; don't answer the door without knowing who's on the other side.

"Make yourself at home," I said, leading him over to the sofa where I proceeded to retrieve all my Friday night snacks and carried them into the kitchen.

I went back into my bedroom without saying another word and started the shower. I climbed in to do just what he said, get myself together. I even washed my hair. I took my time going through my array of toiletries. Then I wrapped my hair in a towel and put on one of my nice robes and went back into the kitchen where I made myself a cup of coffee and some buttered toast. I sat down at my little table without speaking and Michael kept his place on the sofa. I sipped from my cup and took small bites of the toast. When I was finished I went back into my bedroom and closed the door behind me.

I stood at the mirror moisturizing and brushing my hair. It had grown out and the seventies look wasn't working for me so I blew it dry and dug out my flat iron. Once my hair was laid, I carefully applied my make-up, full face, including lip liner and mascara. I got the outfit from the closet that I bought on the day he canceled and put it on. I put on my jewelry and my watch and slipped my feet into a cream-colored pair of strappy mules. I looked good. I looked better than good, I was fly.

That was a good move coming over here without calling but I refused to accept it as checkmate. I hung my alligator skin purse over my shoulder and went out to make my entrance. I was still a player.

"I'm ready," I said, strutting into the living room.

"You look gorgeous," Michael said, admiring me, "You are well worth the wait."

"I'm sorry about that, I wasn't expecting company this morning."

"I don't have any complaints," he said, opening the door.

My eyes squinted at the brightness of the early afternoon sun and I reached in my bag for my sunglasses. I felt the heat of his hand on the small of my back walking down the steps and it stayed warm even when he moved it away. Checkmate. I followed the leader to his car.

"It's a beautiful day, isn't it?" he asked, opening the door of a dark maroon Toyota Avalon.

"Yes, I guess it is," I said, sitting down on the soft leather seat.

"We can grab a quick bite in the mall before the first show starts," Michael said, starting the car, "How does that sound?"

"I'm going with the flow today," I said, feeling relaxed.

Inside the food court I decided on a loaded bake potato and Michael ordered the same. I didn't want to get too full or take a chance on spilling anything on my outfit.

"I'm glad you came," Michael said once we found a table.

"I am too."

"So what was the problem, why didn't you return my phone calls? I wanted to see you."

"I felt like it was going to be us going on a few good dates, you flaking out on me, and me back where I started. I guess

I'm tired of going through the motions."

"I'm going to be fair with you and I want you to be fair with me. I won't hold you accountable for all the women who took advantage of me if you won't hold me accountable for all the guys who did you wrong. We both have jobs and family, things will come up and we will have to handle them. That's life, it's nothing against you."

I couldn't help but laugh because I was guilty, that's what I always did. I guess I did learn that lesson from my mama. In the past it hadn't made much difference, it ended up the same, but this time it might be different.

"That's a good offer. I'll take it," I said, "From this moment on I will only think positive thoughts and give you the benefit of doubt."

"If you forget, I'll remind you," he said, pulling my shades from my face and looking me in the eyes.

"Aren't we here to see a movie?" I asked with a smile.

"Let's do it," he said, cleaning up the table.

Ever the gentleman he took the tray and emptied our trash before we walked down to the theater. When he grabbed my hand I didn't know what to think. I felt awkward but I held on, this was definitely a new experience. We watched a crazy romantic comedy about a guy whose teddy bear had come to life when he was a boy and now they were roommates. I laughed till my eyes watered.

"Thanks for that," I said when we came out, "I haven't laughed that hard in a very long time."

"You're always welcome," he said, putting his arm around my shoulders.

I could feel the heat again and I needed to cool down. Maybe it was a reaction to my lack of male companionship lately.

"Can I treat you to some ice cream?" I asked.

"How can I say no to that, its 85 degrees out here?"

He drove around a few blocks until he found a nice parlor in Buckhead. We got two double dips and found a nearby bench in the shade to sit down and relax. We talked about his work and my work, his family and my family, and then we walked back to the car. Without saying a word he put his arms around me and gave me a big kiss.

"I wanted to wait until I took you home but I couldn't."

My lips were tingling when I said, "You can kiss me again when you take me home."

He smiled and turned up the air conditioner and the radio. He kept his hand around the back of my seat and it made me special. When we got back to my apartment he kissed me again and I don't know about him but I wanted more. Not wanting to be desperate I said my goodbye at the outside of my door. Mama would definitely be proud.

17

Chapter Seventeen

Michael and I saw each other whenever we could for the next three weeks. It wasn't all hot and heavy, more comfortable and fun. He was affectionate but respectful, maybe too respectful for my taste. I couldn't gauge how he felt about me. I probably didn't even know how to be in a relationship without the drama.

I hadn't been home since we met and Mama was on my mind. I needed to see her and I wanted her to meet Michael. I drove over to the store on my way home from work.

"You know I told you about my mama being sick," I said.

"Yeah, is everything all right?"

"Fine as far as I know but with the ways things are I think I should try to visit more often. I was thinking that I'd like for you to meet her. I was hoping this weekend might be good."

"I don't have any plans except for being with you, we can drive up first thing Saturday morning."

"You are a lifesaver, thank you; this means a lot to me."

"I'll call you when I get off," he said, walking me out to my car.

Michael was at the apartment early Saturday before I had

finished getting dressed. I was anxious to get home but I couldn't seem to switch my gears out of slow motion. I hadn't eaten anything since last night but I wasn't hungry.

"Do you mind using the GPS and driving?" I asked after I finally pulled it together.

"No, I'm ready. I haven't been on a road trip in three years."

I dropped down in the passenger seat relieved but my nerves were racked for the whole drive. I was feeling guilty; I hadn't been calling Mama as often as I had before I met Michael. I didn't want her to say anything crazy and embarrass me. I wanted her to recognize me and be happy for me. She had never approved of one guy that I had brought home over the years; she had something bad to say about all of them, I hoped that she would like Michael because I was falling for him.

"I called Daddy and he said we should come by the house first and then we can all ride over to see Mama together," I said, fastening my seatbelt.

"Whatever you want to do, I'm cool," Michael said, being super supportive.

Four hours later we pulled up in front of the house and Daddy was sitting out on the porch waiting. He stood up when he saw it was me in the car.

"Hey, Daddy," I said, walking up to give him a hug.

"Hello, baby, I been missing you around here."

"I was missing y'all too. I want you to meet a good friend of mine, Michael Goodwin."

"Hello, Mr. King, I'm glad to meet you," Michael said, extending his hand.

"Call me Timothy," Daddy replied, shaking his hand. "I'm

glad to know that Tia has somebody to look out for her down there in Atlanta. I worry about her sometimes."

"Don't worry, sir; I'll take care of her."

"Okay then," he said. "Well, let's go and see your mama. Maybe we can take her out to lunch."

"I hope so, Daddy, I can't get used to her being at that place."

"She's all right, baby, she's more relaxed there."

"If you'll give me the address, I'll drive," Michael said.

I got in the backseat so Daddy could direct him to the facility. I needed a minute by myself in the back to ask God to let my mama know me and be in a good mood.

I took a deep breath when we got there and Michael grabbed my hand as we walked in through the double doors.

"Is Samantha King in her room?" Daddy asked the young woman named Terry at the front desk.

"I think she's in the dining room," Terry said with a smile.

Michael and I trailed Daddy down the hallway and I was feeling like I was about to faint. From the entrance to the dining room I could see Mama and she looked good. Her hair was freshly combed and she was even wearing lipstick.

"Sammie, look who's here to see you," Daddy said, patting Mama on her arm, "It's Tia."

"Hey, Mama, how have you been doing?" I asked, giving her a hug and kiss.

"We came to take you out to lunch, honey," Daddy said.

"We're getting ready to eat lunch here," Mama replied, getting annoyed. "Why do I need to go out somewhere else? Y'all can eat here if you want."

"That makes sense, we'll do just that," Daddy said, nodding

for us to sit down at the table.

"Who's the guy, Tia, is he your husband?" she asked, making fun of me.

"Mama," I said embarrassed, wanting to put my hand over her mouth.

"Hello, Mrs. King, I'm Michael Goodwin, a close friend of your daughter."

"It's nice to meet you, Michael," she said, leaning forward and staring at him, "Do you have a job, are you married, and do you have any children?"

"No, ma'am, I've never been married and I don't have any children, but I do have a job," Michael said, trying not to smile. "Tia asked me the same things when we met."

"That's good, she's met her share of bums."

"All of us have," Michael said.

"You're right about that," Mama replied.

"What's on the menu?" Daddy asked, changing the subject.

"It doesn't matter," Mama answered, "It all tastes the same to me."

Daddy ordered a plate but Michael and I passed. I was starving but I couldn't eat. I was so uncomfortable sitting there since Mama had her claws out. I wanted her to like Michael and I wanted him to like her too but they weren't even talking.

"I think I'm going to take myself a nap," Mama said when she'd finished.

"I'll go with you to your room, Mama," I said, standing up.

I pushed the chair out of the dining room and down the hallway trying to think of something to say that would make the connection I needed from her but my mind was blank.

"I want to sit in my lazyboy, Tia," she said when we got inside her room. "Turn on the TV for me, I think one of my shows is on."

I helped her out of the wheel chair and into her lazyboy recliner before I picked up the remote and turned on the TV.

"Close the blinds for me too, chile."

I sat down on the small sofa beside her and asked, "Do you need anything else, Mama?"

"Uh- uh, except that seems like a good man out there, try to hold onto him, you hear."

"Yes, Mama," I said, feeling the slight burn of tears in my eyes.

"Go on now, I'm tired. Call me sometime."

I wanted to put my arms around her and lay there for a while but I knew she wouldn't let me. That wasn't our way. Besides, I had gotten what I came for, her approval. Daddy and Michael were waiting in the hallway when I came out. We walked out past Terry and through the double doors without saying a word. It was always hard walking out without my mama. Daddy directed Michael back to the house even though I'm sure he remembered the way.

"We're hungry Daddy, I haven't had anything to eat today," I said when we stopped in front of the house.

"Do you want me to fix you something, baby?"

"No, I think we'll go over to Sonic."

"Are you two going to stay at the house tonight?" Daddy asked.

"No, we're going to go ahead and drive back, I have a lot to do before Monday morning. I just had Mama on my mind and wanted to see her."

"All right, baby, call me when you get in off the road."

"I will, bye, Daddy," I said, giving him a hug on the porch the same way I did when we arrived. "I'll drive us back," I said, walking towards the driver's side with my hand out for the keys.

"That's okay, I'm not tired," Michael said, walking me back around to the passenger side.

I was emotionally drained so I was content he didn't mind driving back.

"You okay?" he asked after we got in the car.

"I'm good, I just wish you could have met her before all this happened."

"I'm glad I came today. She's all right, she reminds me of my mama and grandma."

"She's old school," I said, offering an excuse.

"So am I," he laughed, "My birthday is next Friday, one more year and I'll be the big 5-0.

My lips stayed sealed because I didn't even want to speak the words of how old I would be on my next birthday.

18

Chapter Eighteen

When Michael told me his birthday was coming up I made plans to cook him an outstanding dinner. I couldn't make up my mind whether to go gourmet or soul food to the heart. Then I came up with my plan to mix the two. That wasn't the only thing I planned to heat up. In my pledge to boycott men I had the greatest intentions and I was dedicated, but the flesh is weak. I don't know why I'm so hot-blooded or where I get it from, I don't think Mama has had anything to do with Daddy for over 15 years.

I made a meatloaf in honor of the ground beef that had brought us together and then I found some recipes for creamed spinach, summer squash, and whipped potatoes seasoned with parmesan and chives. For dessert I made a devil's food chocolate cake. I changed into a sexy black dress that I bought specifically for tonight. It was shorter than anything I would wear outside of the house but I had no plans of going anywhere.

"Happy Birthday," I said, greeting him at the door.

"You look so good I can't ask for anything else today," he said, eyeing me up and down.

"Not after I slaved over the stove all day, you are going to eat."

"Don't worry; I brought my appetite, so let's see if you have any talent in the kitchen.

"You're going to eat those words before dessert," I said, self-assured. "Come on in the kitchen, the food is ready to put on the table."

"Your place looks like you lived here for years," he said on the way to the kitchen.

"I've been dragging this furniture around with me for a long time, I even sold some things when I moved out of my last apartment."

"That's one of the differences between men and women, my house was practically empty for almost a year after I moved in."

"We ladies need all of our stuff to be comfortable at home," I said, showing him to his seat at the table.

He sat there quietly watching me as I placed the food in serving bowls before I sat them on the table. I avoided his eyes as I filled two glasses with ice and took out the pitcher of sweet tea and set them on the table. The final touch was to light the tall white candle in the middle of the table that I kept for show. Pleased with my arrangement I sat down across from Michael.

"I blessed the food when you cooked for me, would you like to do the honors over this meal?"

"Not particularly, but I will if you want me to."

"I want you to," I said, bowing my head.

"Lord, bless this food and the hands that prepared it, amen."

It wasn't what I had expected but it was better than some

others I had heard over the years so I said, "Amen."

"Now to see if it tastes as good as it looks and smells."

"Do I look like I can't cook?"

"No you don't, but you could be eating take-out," he said, slicing his meatloaf.

"Since you're a guest and it's your birthday I'm going to let that slide today."

"I'm just teasing you," he said with his mouth full, "It's better than my mama's and that says a lot because she can burn."

"Thank you, I took special care on this dinner. I even dug out one of my cookbooks."

"I didn't know I had it like that," he said, finishing his plate.

"Don't get the big head, but I've enjoyed the time that we've spent together and I wanted to show you how much I appreciate it," I said, getting up to clear the table.

"Aside from the hard time you gave me in the beginning, you're good company."

"I explained my handicap to you already, I have trust issues."

"We're past that aren't we?"

"I believe we are," I said, taking his hand and leading him to the living room, "However, there are some things we haven't had a meeting of the minds on yet."

Michael took a seat on the couch and I turned on my music system to play a slow R&B CD that Wayne had made for me. I sat down close beside him and looked him in the eyes.

"I wasn't planning on a long discussion," he said, putting his arms around my shoulders and pulling me close for long hot kiss while he unzipped my dress.

"Now we're on the same page," I said before I kissed him

deep in his mouth.

He was a lot more passionate than I thought he would be. We got busy right there on the sofa and it was more than I expected in every way.

"Can we take this to the bedroom?" he whispered in my ear.

Somebody needed to play Prince's "Adore" because I was way gone. The whole thing was freaky, sensuous, and sweet. Damn, this was the man I'd been waiting for.

"Would you mind if I stayed over?" he asked, kissing me on the cheek an hour later.

"There's no way I'm going to let you leave," I answered.

The next morning I kept my eyes closed feeling awkward and self-conscious as he moved his hands over the hills, valleys, and folding terrain of my body when he simply said, "You know I want to marry you."

My eyes flew wide open but my ears were straining to hear the words again, "Don't play with me like that."

"I'm not playing with you, Tia. If I wasn't serious about you I wouldn't be here. I'm in love with you. The question is how do you feel, do you want to marry me?"

"Hell yeah, absofuckinglutely, you better believe it!" I thought to myself, but my lips simply said, "Yes, I do."

"I knew I was going to ask you the first day I saw you in the store. You looked like the woman I always imagined I'd be married to."

It wasn't exactly how I dreamed the moment would be. I thought I would be seventy pounds lighter in a royal blue dress sitting in a romantic restaurant where the waiter serves me a glass of champagne with the ring sparkling at the bottom as he gets down on one knee. He leaned over and kissed me and I kissed him back and neither of us had brushed our teeth, but it was perfect. After another half hour of morning smashing we showered and made breakfast together. I felt like I was already a married woman. When he left, I couldn't get Jazz on the phone fast enough.

"Girl, I found him," I shouted into the receiver.

"Found who?" she asked, totally oblivious.

"I met this guy at the grocery store near my apartment about three months ago. We've been seeing each other and long story short we're getting married."

"Tia, you are going to have to back that up, way back, all the way back to the beginning. You haven't said anything about meeting a guy since Heavy E."

"You're wrong for that, Jazz, that's why I didn't say anything. I was tired of getting all geeked up about some dude and then later regretting the whole thing. I decided I wasn't going to say anything until it got serious."

"It sounds like it has been serious before now."

"Are you happy for me or what?" I said impatiently.

"I'm sorry, I'm very happy for you, I just don't want to see you get hurt again."

"Didn't I tell you, he wants to marry me?"

"Excuse me for being slow this morning but I didn't see this one coming."

"Honestly, I didn't either. He's ten years older than me, but I swear he's the one."

"I'm not going to say I told you so about that age thing."

"I'll give you that one. I'm with Anita Baker, baby, *Caught up in the Rapture*, and I didn't settle. I have a decent job and I have a man who loves and treats me like his queen."

"Thank God, Tia, but it sounds more like Etta James' *At Last* to me."

"For real, Jazz, that's not funny."

"Yes it is, and I know you have to go and blow up all your girls' phones with the news."

"And you know this, bye, and thanks for being my friend."

"What do you mean, friend, I know I'm the matron of honor."

"Without a doubt, Jazz, without a doubt."

I set my alarm for 5:00 on Monday morning to call all my girls.

"Denise, Yvonne, get everybody on conference call, because it's my turn to stand in front of the preacher, I'm getting married."

"To who?" Denise asked, "You haven't told us about anybody."

"My fiancé's name is Michael Goodwin."

"Excuse me, Miss Thang," Yvonne said.

"That will be Mrs. Thang to you, girl, and believe me when I tell you payback is a big mean dog with long teeth. I want all of you bridezillas to be bridesmaids in my wedding and I don't want to hear any excuses."

"Congratulations, Tia," Denise said, "You know we will."

"Yeah, we'll be there for you girlfriend," Yvonne added.

I was so happy I couldn't go back to sleep. Dr. Tia King was soon to become Mrs. Tia Goodwin. My phone rang just as I was about to get up. I thought it was one of my girls calling to say they had heard the news but when I looked at the number it was Reggie.

I pushed answer and said, "Reggie, do me a favor, lose my number. I'm getting married."

CPSIA information can be obtained at www.ICGtesting.com
Printed in the USA
LVOW10s0825071214

417612LV00001B/3/P